SEAMS OF THE INFINITE

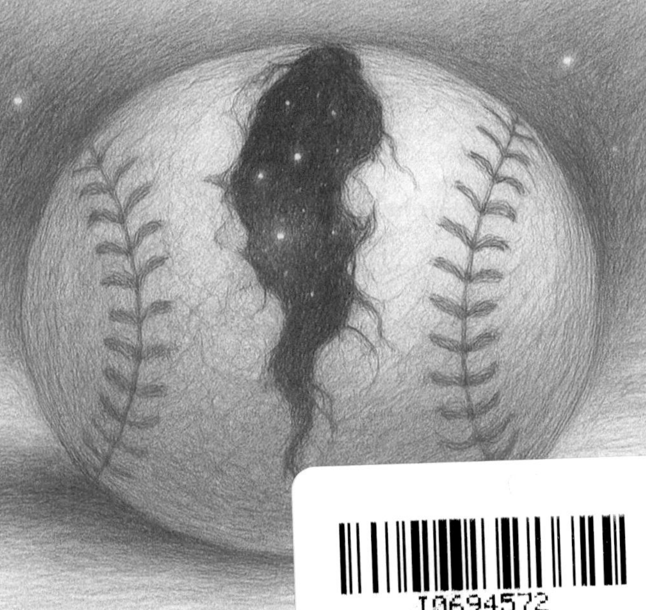

Lacandon Jungle Press
www.LJPBooks.com

First Edition: 2026
Paperback ISBN: 978-1-967354-07-8

eBook ISBN: 978-1-967354-08-5

For Shawn

You had a gift
Not for fixing what was broken,
but for making it bearable.

When the world turned heavy,
you leaned in with that look, that grin,
and dropped it like a lifeline:
"Why am I not surprised?"

You cracked the sky with humor
and carved space in the silence
where the rest of us could breathe.

Wherever you are now
beyond the noise, beyond the nonsense
I hope you are still saying it,
still catching someone off guard
with that same sly grace.

You were a brother.
You still are.
Always.

Thank You

Thank you to the legends –
those who survived, spoke up, and pitched through pressure
most people could not name.
Men who played the game with a target on their back and
still found a way to rise.
Their courage stitched seams into history that can still be
traced with a fingertip.

And to those who saw the seams before I did
the friends, mentors, storytellers, and quiet prophets who
taught me to look past the surface.
You helped me see how a story moves beneath the one people think they are reading.
You taught me what it means to listen between the lines.

To the families who carried these stories forward,
to the players who gave us their joy, their flaws, and their
truth,
and to the communities who kept the memory alive when
the record books fell silent
this book stands on your shoulders.

To the ones I lost along the way
whose voices echo in the corners of every chapter
your humor, your fire, and your hard-earned wisdom guided

more than the writing.
You guided the man doing the writing.

    To the readers who walk into the Dark Archives with

open eyes

thank you for stepping into the shadows with me.
May you find something worth carrying back into the light.

Contents

Foreword

I first met Billy Graves when my husband George and I guested on his podcast, Slasher Sports Cinema. We had just made our first feature, the horror-comedy Obstacle Corpse, about a mudder-style race where half the athletes have been invited to be killed. Graves was engaged and kind, and he loved the film, which endeared him to me immediately. What impressed me first and most was his generous spirit. After that, it was his passion for both genre and sports.

The idea of a combined horror and sports podcast is unusual, but should it be? Each contains thrills, people you root for and even love, and outcomes that feel larger than life. Both sports and horror invoke incredible passion in people. Certainly in Billy, and it was not simple fanaticism. It was love and unquenchable interest in understanding and appreciating both.

It came as no surprise to me that his first full length genre piece would blend those two sources of inspiration, creativity, and wonder. *Seams of the Infinite* is a work of speculative beauty, bearing not only a depth of baseball knowledge entirely unseen in genre fiction, but also an aching social conscience and authentic sense of period detail.

In early Summer of 1970, Pittsburgh Pirate right hander Dock Ellis pitched a no-hitter. Those games are certainly uncommon enough to celebrate, but Ellis's feat was even more noteworthy. He had taken LSD a few hours earlier. This is not your run of the mill underdog sports story, but in Graves's hands, the tale transcends sports altogether.

Graves knows the game itself, June 12, 1970, facing the Padres in San Diego, down to pitch. He uses the numbers, the statistics, and the tidy box score as both a foundation and a metaphor. Here are the parameters. These are the rules. Play the game. In Graves's hands, Ellis is playing against something bigger than the San Diego Padres, playing for something more profound than the Pittsburgh Pirates.

Graves's knowledge of and passion for the game ground the supernatural elements of his tale, elements tinged by Lovecraft almost as much as by Serling. Fittingly trippy, the imagery delivers a breathing nightmare. There is a music to Graves's words, a rhythm to his sentences that hypnotizes.

What I found in *Seams of the Infinite* was a dark poetry. The Dock Ellis of Billy Graves's imagination may not change the rules of the game, one crafted to keep people who look like Ellis in check. But he challenges his own cosmic insignificance, and in the middle ground between light and shadow, that is a monstrous feat.

—Hope Madden, author of Killer Pictures, director of Obstacle Corpse

Introduction

You are about to enter a story that belongs to two countries at once.
The first is the United States you know. The one that sells popcorn at ballparks and calls its games innocent. The one that loves its myths clean and its heroes simpler than they ever were. A nation that believes it can explain itself with a flag, a handshake, and nine innings played under fair skies.

The second country hides inside the first one.
Its streets are familiar but the shadows run longer. Its history is louder if you bother to listen. It is a place where the rules are older than law and colder than justice. A place where a man can stand on a mound in perfect daylight and still feel the night reaching for him. This other America has no anthem. It does not sing. It hums under its breath and waits.

Tonight's story takes place where those two countries touch. Dock Ellis stood there once. A pitcher with a fastball that broke late and a temper that broke early. A man who carried both defiance and fear in the same pocket. On the day he threw his no hitter, he was high enough to see the seams on the world as clearly as the seams on the ball. The country he lived in told him the game was simple. The country beneath it showed him the truth.

Some stories are born clean.
This is not one of them.

This one comes to you after being scraped out of the Dark Archives, a place where the record books fade and the real accounts echo. Here the score does not lie. Here the umpires wear faces that may not be human. Here the rules stretch from the strike zone to the edge of the universe, because someone out there is always keeping count.

You are free to believe what you like.
Maybe Dock just pitched the game of his life and nothing more.
Maybe the acid twisted every sight and sound.
Maybe what he saw in the corners of his vision was nothing more than shadow and pressure.
Maybe the country is kinder than the mirror it holds up to itself.

Or maybe not.
Maybe the truth is exactly what Dock saw.
A world stitched together by hands we never see, held in place by rules we never learned, and tilted just enough that some men spend their whole lives pitching uphill.

So take your seat. Settle in.
The field is chalked. The lights are warm.
The sky above San Diego is clear enough that you might think something is watching.

In a moment you will hear the first pitch.
Whether you call it a strike or a warning is your choice.
Stories, like games, do not wait for permission.

When the seams of the infinite start to split, you can only decide whether to look away or keep your eyes open.

This is the record we recovered.
This is what Dock saw.
What you see is up to you.

Chapter One

The Devil Made Me Do It

The ceiling fan whirred overhead like a military helicopter, yet its breeze was scarcely noticeable while lying on the queen-sized bed. It was hot, muggy, and being early morning made no difference to the Los Angeles summer. Still, he wasn't pitching today, so Dock decided to take a trip. Not like a hidden destination or to grandma's house. This trip was different and wouldn't require him to leave his hotel room.

Dock had fallen asleep with the television still glowing, a soft square of light humming in the dark motel room. Flip Wilson had been on. *The Flip Wilson Show* was brand-new, everybody was talking about it. Dock had laughed himself half to sleep, Geraldine cracking wise in that high voice, hips swinging, "The devil made me do it." America loved it. Black, white, young, old; they all tuned in. A Black man in a dress could make the whole country howl.

But Dock knew it wasn't just laughs. Flip was sharp. He was slipping jabs past the guard, showing the absurdity of it all. Dock thought about how Geraldine was welcome in living rooms across America while Black kids in Oakland were getting beat down for raising a fist. Flip was the salve; the Panthers were the wound.

The night before had played in his head like a flickering reel: Geraldine telling a joke, Arthur Ashe raising his racket, Nixon sweating under the lights, Kent State students falling to the ground. The laugh track bled into the sound of gunfire; applause turned to sirens. Dock was caught between the two screens. One was a country laughing itself stupid, the other tearing at the seams.

Dock muttered to no one, *"Different rules for us. Always different rules."*

And lying there, somewhere between booze, smoke, and the acid that was just starting to creep, Dock couldn't tell where Flip's punchlines ended and his own thoughts began. Maybe comedy was a drug, too. Maybe America needed it as bad as he did.

He leaned back, eyelids heavy, letting the static fold into the hum of the fan, the rhythm of his pulse. The trip was warming up, his senses sharpening like a needle on vinyl. Every sound had weight, every flicker of light a story.

His eyelids weighed tons. They were the weight of distant planets and he let himself drift.

A cigarette smoldered in an ashtray filled with half-chewed gum. The gray smoke rose and curled; almost shaping itself into a cobra that looked him in the eye. He blew at it weakly, and it dissolved into nothing.

"God damn, man. Just looking at the smoke makes it feel 10 degrees hotter in this place." Dock thought to himself.

The room smelled of sweat and old cologne. His travel clothes as always were wrinkled slacks and a polo that smelled of stale sweat which were piled on the chair like a body he'd already abandoned.

The acid he'd dropped a half hour ago was starting to smudge the room's edges, as if the walls were chalk lines scuffed by too many spikes. Corners curled in on themselves, colors bleeding past their borders. But it wasn't enough. Not for today. Not for the kind of day that demanded extra innings.

He slid another tab from his wallet and laid it on his tongue. Bitter as aspirin, sharp as a foul tip off the mask. It dissolved fast, fizzing against the roof of his mouth, and left a taste like copper and paper, the ghost of blood and newsprint. His jaw clenched on instinct. A film of sweat broke over his upper lip, salty, metallic.

Almost immediately, the air thickened. The hum of the ceiling fan slowed, each rotation dragging like a long windup. His heartbeat ticked in his ears. It was not steady, not human, but the hollow thud of a ball hitting a mitt, again and again. Restlessness crawled under his skin, electric, like he'd been plugged into a socket. He rubbed his arms as if to scratch it out, but the itch wasn't on the surface. It was deeper.

Dock muttered to the empty room, a cracked grin forming: "Gonna need more than nine today." He rubbed his aching head, stabbing pain just behind his left eye. "Just a little something," he whispered, as if trying to convince himself. But the room pulsed in rhythm with his heartbeat, a dissonant drum that called to something buried deep within him. Shadows flickered in the corners of his vision, retreating whenever he turned his head, but he could swear they were watching.

Dock pulled himself from the bed, stumbling into action by a force beyond comprehension, staggering past empty bottles as if they were landmines scattered across a battlefield. Their glassy throats caught the light, winking like tiny watchful eyes. Each crunch beneath his heel felt like the crack of a bat on bone.

The carpet swelled under his bare feet, soft and pulsing, alive with its own heartbeat. He swayed, half convinced he was trudging through the outfield grass at Forbes Field, only now the blades screamed his name with every step. Sweat rolled down his brow and into the corner of his mouth, briny and metallic, like the taste of a split lip. The LSD did not just sharpen the senses. It bent them, stretched them, made every sound too loud and every color too bright. Every touch became both velvet and sandpaper at once.

He pawed for his suitcase by the door and found it already zipped, squared away like somebody else had been here preparing him. It mocked him with its readiness, daring him to believe he was still in control. "Fuck man, what you been doing? Packing in your sleep?"

The door lets out a mournful groan as it swings open, the sound echoing off the tiled walls of the bathroom and making him flinch. The hinges squeal in protest, as if they too are exhausted from years of use. It's a sound that sends a chill down his spine, like fingers running down a chalkboard.

He caught glimpses of himself splintered in the mirror. The eyes staring back were wild, bloodshot, a landscape of confusion. His reflection lagged, a half-second behind reality, its mouth still agape while his own had moved on to wonder if it was really there at all. A specter mimicking his every move but always a breath late. "Dock, you a good lookin' muthafucka, but right now you better get straight."

"Too much, just too damn much," he said, shaking his head as the mirror-reflection did the same, a beat too slow to catch up with him. Dock fought through the fog, his stomach rolling. "What the hell happened last night?" The words slipped out like a bad pitch, wild and unrefined.

Each step sent shudders through his spine, and he staggered slightly, brushing his palms against the countertop to steady himself. The bathroom linoleum below felt cold, its slickness a sharp contrast to the heat radiating from his skin. He could almost feel the ground shifting under him, an earthquake of consciousness echoing through his bones.

The water ran frigid but gave him a moment's clarity. The chill spread from his hands to his neck, the way ice melts in bourbon. He let it pour over his face in handfuls, desperate for it to bite deeper, to freeze him back into himself. Droplets slid down his forehead, into his eyes, stinging sharp as smoke.

For half a breath the world snapped into focus. White tile, chipped sink, the dull hum of plumbing. Then it slipped again. The edges blurred and colors bled. He gripped the porcelain with both hands until his knuckles whitened, but the sink felt soft and pliant, like wet clay under his palms.

The haze wrapped around him like a warm uniform fresh from the dryer, clinging close and comforting in its weight. The towel on his shoulder anchored him as he let the high rise, wave after wave, carrying him anywhere but here.

A shrill ring shattered the room, cutting through his haze like a foul tip off the mask. It was not a gentle knock or a drifting sound. It was the rotary phone on the nightstand, loud and insistent, each ring clanging like a bell in his skull. Dock's head turned slow, dreamlike, the noise dragging him back up from the ocean he had been sinking into.

"Dock?"

The voice came first in his head, like a whisper. Then reality caught up: the *ring* of the rotary phone on the nightstand. The sound drilled through the walls, each ring stretching longer, bending like a warped record. Why did he hear his own name being called? He hadn't answered, yet answering was inevitable.

Dock crawled over the queen bed and yanked the receiver off the cradle. The coiled cord writhed like a worm in hot ash between his fingers. He pressed the weight of it against his ear.

The voice spilled through the line, distant and shimmering, like it had traveled a hundred years to reach him. A woman's voice, familiar, warm.

"You're something else," she said, a soft shake in her words. "How does it groove with you to drop acid first thing in the morning when you've got a start to make? I can *hear* it in you, Dock."

A lazy grin spread across his face, eyes half-closed as if in a waking dream. "I'm not even supposed to be here," he chuckled, laugh bubbling up like a fresh Double Cola.

His laughter came again, hollow and echoing in the empty corridor of his mind. Her words were a distant hum, lost in the swirling currents of the fan's rhythm - Almost like white noise. "Wait, what did you just say?" His heart skipped a beat, a sudden jolt in the dreamscape.

"You heard me. Game 1 in San Diego starts in about 8 hours and you're in L.A. messing with them tabs."

The words cut sharper than they should have. Harder than any fastball he'd ever introduced to any batter crowding the plate. "You know you're pitching today, right?"

Dock Ellis, the Pirates' live-wire right-hander, the one who strutted as loud off the field as he did on it, was not supposed to be pitching today. At least that is what he thought when he lit up last night. He was the kind of pitcher who thrived on chaos, swaggering through lineups with more attitude than command, but he still needed the armor of preparation. LSD had no place in his game-day ritual.

If the schedule had shifted and he was the man on the mound, then he was about to walk into a start unmoored, high as Saturn's rings, carrying not just a team but his own reputation, the one that said Dock Ellis could talk big and still back it up. Now, for the first time, he was not sure if he could.

The words twisted and danced, morphing into abstract shapes in his mind. Reality wavered, a mirage on the horizon, as tension coiled like a snake in the pit of his stomach. How did he lose an entire day? A 5-man pitching rotation is like clockwork and the clock was striking for Dock.

"I don't know what you need to do to shake that haze, but baby you'd better do it."

Her voice wasn't the same as before. It was. But it wasn't. The tab twisted everything, bent her tone like a record warped in the sun.

"Baby, you know me. I could pitch with one eye closed," Dock said, though even as the words left him, he knew he'd bitten off more than he could chew. He'd have to prove it, and the thought made his chest tighten.

"The hell you can. Dave Roberts ain't pitching blind today, so you'd best get your head clear."

She said it sharp, a jab straight to the ribs. Comparison was a thief of joy, and right then it was a sobering thought to a man whose mind was swimming. Dock muttered, "Dave Roberts ain't got shit on me." He tried to play it cool, but cool felt far away, another city and another ballpark.

Dock rubbed his face, trying to trace the hours back like following baselines, but the chalk lines blew away in the wind. When had he dropped that first tab? Last night? This morning? The acid stretched time until it snapped, each minute an extra inning with no scoreboard to tell him where he stood. The calendar in his mind flipped backward, an exasperated rewind, but no answers came. Reality slipped like sand through his fingers, and when it fell through, it left him empty-handed.

He sat up, slow and laboring, the edges of the room cutting into him like shards of glass. His voice strained, thin as fishing line trying to bridge the distance between delirium and fact. "But it wasn't my goddamn day."

"It is now," she said, her words suddenly crystallizing with cruel clarity. "And you're way out of state."

There are two kinds of goodbyes on a wall phone: the soft click of a gentle hang-up, and the sharp report of a receiver slammed into its cradle. Dock heard the latter. The slam cracked through the receiver like a bat finding sweet pine, echoing in his ear long after the line went dead. He held the phone out, heavy as a brick, as if it had been used to club him.

The silence that followed wasn't empty. It hissed, alive, curling around him like smoke, as though the walls themselves were listening. Somewhere behind his eyes, laughter played back but not his, not hers, but Flip Wilson's, smooth and sly from last night's TV haze. *The devil made me do it.* Geraldine's voice, all sass and sparkle, but now warped, echoing like it had been meant for him all along.

Dock set the receiver back in its cradle, slow, like it might bite him. His pulse thudded in his neck, hot and ragged. Eight hours. L.A. to San Diego. And a start he hadn't seen coming.

The devil made me do it. Maybe that's why he dropped the tab. Maybe that's why he couldn't claw free from the fog. Maybe that's why, in a few short hours, he'd be standing on a mound with the world watching.

The acid was blooming now, a cruel flower unfurling behind his eyes. Colors snapped sharp, then bled at the edges. Shadows twitched like they wanted to step free. The carpet rippled when he moved, the wall swayed when he touched it. There was no off switch. No rewind. No way back.

He staggered toward the door, clutching the wall to steady himself, every step both weightless and heavy. His mouth was dry, but the words scraped out anyway. "Alright," he whispered, though no one was there to hear it. "Let's see if a man can pitch blind."

The knob turned beneath his hand, cold and real against the unreality blooming in his veins. Beyond it, the morning waited, unknowing, the hours ticking down toward a game that would not forgive him.

And with that, Dock Ellis stepped into the day that would haunt baseball forever.

CHAPTER TWO

The City Watches Back

The door shut behind Dock with a heavy click, a sound that echoed in his chest more than the hallway. His senses still spiked. He straightened the lapels of his jacket and tugged his cuffs smooth. Crisp shirt, pressed trousers, shoes polished to catch the sun; clothes cut like armor. But the cleaner he looked, the sharper the stares seemed to cut.

No matter how fine the outfit, Dock felt naked under the city's gaze. Shop windows, passing strangers, even shadows seemed to watch him. He was high enough to scrape the cosmos, every nerve lit like a star. It was the trip, he told himself, but that did not make the weight of it any lighter. Dock Ellis did not do plain. He never had. You stepped into Los Angeles looking like you mattered or you did not step out at all. This attention did not feel like it did in Pittsburgh. It did not feel like the paranoia of a euphoric high. It felt different.

A bus thundered past, brakes squealing, and Dock caught the poster slashed along its side. LOVE STORY. A pretty boy and girl pressed forehead to forehead, words bold under them: Love means never having to say you are sorry. The phrase stuck in his head like gum on a cleat. Never having to say sorry. Dock muttered the line under his breath, trying it out, hearing how it bent and echoed in the trip. It did not sound like love to him. It sounded like someone getting away with something.

He watched the bus grind away, the lovers' faces bending across its windows, the slogan stretching thin as taffy. For a moment it felt like the city itself was whispering at him. Do not say sorry, Dock. Not today.

The sidewalk jittered with movement. Women with shopping bags, men in gray suits, kids licking ice cream cones. Dock adjusted his cap and started across, joining the tide of bodies under the white signal.

Halfway through, a horn spat. The crosswalk stripes blurred into chalked baselines. He kept his pace, head up, as if jogging between innings.

"Hey. You. Stop right there."

Two uniforms peeled from the corner like shadows stepping off a wall.

The first was thick as a barricade, mirrored aviators swallowing his eyes, badge throwing back the sun. **Sgt. J. Braddock.** His stance said trouble before his mouth said a word.

The second trailed a step behind, lean and wired too tight. His badge read **Officer T. Keene.** Young. Nervous.

Dock blinked, the outside world still spinning and pulsing. Braddock's aviators stretched wide like dinner plates, the sun bending off the badge in a strobe. Dock tried to steady his breath. Hold it together, Dock. Straight lines, not spirals.

Braddock's gaze dragged down Dock's suit, slow and deliberate. "Well, don't you look dapper," he said. His smile was crooked. "Funny thing, though. I did not see a crosswalk where you came from."

Dock's tongue felt thick. Words came delayed, as if they had to fight through molasses to reach daylight. "Light was white. Same as for everyone else. Guess you missed them." He nodded at the white pedestrians already halfway down the block.

Braddock's lip curled. "I did not ask about them. I asked about you. Now let me see some identification."

Dock's pulse jumped. He wanted to hold the line and spit the words that circled in his head like gospel. Fourth Amendment. Probable cause. Rights are not just for white men in ties. His mouth opened, and the words tumbled out, jumbled in his own mind but far too clear to the men in front of him.

"I do not have to show you anything unless I have committed a crime. Fourth Amendment says so."

That got Keene's throat working, a half-swallowed twitch of nerves. Braddock just chuckled, low and mean.

"Big words," Braddock said. "...for a sidewalk lawyer. But when a shopkeeper says some fella's hanging near his door, making customers nervous? That's probable cause."

Dock squinted at the drugstore across the street. The sign bent, letters sliding down like paint in the rain: *DRUGS* flickering, then nothing. People walked in and out, no hesitation, no fear. His voice came out rough. "Sidewalk's public. Not loitering. Not a crime. You know that."

Braddock leaned closer, mirrored shades warping Dock's reflection into something insect-like. "You wanna keep lawyering me, or you wanna explain it downtown?"

Dock's mouth went dry. He thought of Manny's voice, steady behind the plate. Focus. Fire it in here, Dock. He wanted to dig in and stand firm, but his hands had already betrayed him. They were fishing for his wallet as if they belonged to someone else, moving without permission, moving the way men move when they know the rules are written for somebody else.

He pulled out his ID. The plastic felt too hot, edges curling under his fingertips. He handed it over, swallowing the bile in his throat.

Braddock held it too long, smirk widening. "Ellis. Dock Phillip Ellis Jr. Well now... lookie here." He passed it back slow, like returning something he owned. "Guess I was right to ask. You ballplayers think a uniform makes you untouchable?"

Dock shoved the ID into his pocket, jaw tight. "Uniform's not the problem here. Or maybe it is, huh?"

Braddock ignored it. "You walk careful, Ellis. A man in your shoes ought to know paper rights don't always fit the sidewalk."

Keene shifted, eyes darting away. He looked like he wanted to vanish into the pavement cracks.

Braddock gave Dock one last smirk, then signaled for Keene to follow. They walked off slow, like they'd just taught a lesson.

Dock stood still, hands shaking though he forced them steady.

A yellow cab slid up to the curb. Dock climbed inside, the world outside still melting, still bending wrong.

The cab door clapped shut and the vinyl seat clung like it had hands. Dock shifted, but the material pulled at his shirt, peeling away in slow rips, sticky as Velcro. For a second he thought of Braddock again, the detention the sergeant could not get him with. Maybe the universe had decided to pin him down instead.

The air was heavy with smells too harsh to ignore. Leather soured with sweat. Old tobacco clung like stale ghosts. Gasoline threaded in from the vents. Each scent cut him thin and pressed a headache deep at the back of his skull. He blinked, but the pressure only grew.

Through the partition glass, the driver's face warped and stretched like melted wax, then snapped back to normal. Nose, jaw, eyes. All fine again. Ordinary.

Dock was not convinced.

And still, Braddock's voice rolled around the cab like it owned the place: *"Untouchable"*. The syllables echoed tighter in this confined box, as if the name itself could shut the doors on him. "Only untouchables are those jive ass motherfuckers behind the badge."

"Airport," the driver said. Not a question. A verdict, as if there was no other choice.

Dock nodded once, relieved to be away from the outside, if only separated by a window.

The driver's eyes flicked to the mirror. "Don't miss the signs," he muttered. Soft, almost to himself.

Dock stiffened. Signs. Could've meant traffic signs. Could've meant the scoreboard, the hand-flash of Manny Sanguillén crouched low. Could've meant something else entirely. He told himself it was just the acid, just his head rerouting words into omens.

Outside, the world streamed past in staccato bursts, the city flicking by at a speed just above what the mind could process and half a beat off what the senses could trust. Skyscraper windows flashed teeth, then vanished behind the next rolling wall of sunlight. A construction worker hoisted his sign and, for a split-second, the orange triangle radiated like a warning beacon from some alien language. The cab's momentum chewed through everything, block after block, while the city's messages howled for his attention, then disintegrated on contact.

Billboards leered from the sides of buildings, their slogans molten and mutating in Dock's vision. The LOVE STORY ad again, only now the man's face bled into the woman's, their features collapsing and reconstituting with each passing pole; the tagline slid apart, splitting into Sorry. Never Sorry. Always Sorry, every permutation a jab between Dock's ribs. He blinked, but the words stuck, the stubborn afterimage burned into his brain. Next a neon sign over a dry cleaner's, OPEN, letters stuttering in the haze, flickered until it only read OMEN. Dock gripped the seat tighter, knuckles going white in the shadowed cab.

He stared at the sidewalk's edge, where pedestrians poured down the blocks in jerky, animated fragments. A girl in a yellow dress, then five men in the same gray suit, then the girl again, her dress now streaked with something red, or maybe that was just the afterglow of a brake light. He could not tell what was bleeding into what, but the repetition made it feel like the city was stuck in a loop and he was the only one who noticed.

A pawn shop's window display snapped into focus: a pyramid of televisions, each set to a different channel, all tuned to the same man in a navy blue suit. The man was talking, gesturing, but the sounds were replaced by static and the image kept freezing with his mouth wide. Above, the sign screamed in block capitals: WE BUY GOD. Dock's mind refused the message, tried to reboot, so the sign glitched and reset: WE BURY GOD. The words made no sense, then perfect sense, then vanished as fast as they'd punched through the glass. Dock craned his neck to see if it would return, but the city had already eaten the store and replaced it with the blank face of a chain pharmacy.

The cab picked up speed. The sidewalk blurred, then reassembled into a parade of mothers, shoppers, and school kids. Each face melted into the next, sometimes literally, as if the flesh were soft clay and an invisible hand was smearing away the details. Dock blinked hard and tried to clear the double vision, but the city was doubling down. It was not relenting. Every window reflected not only his face but every face he had ever worn, every mask he had lifted for the press, the team, and the world. He sucked in air, but the air was thick, the molecules pressed so tight together that it hurt to pull them into his lungs.

The taxi shot past an intersection, and for a moment Dock saw the far corner transform into a baseball diamond. Literal bases, chalked and bright, with four men in suits pacing the lines. The men moved in perfect sync, their hats low and their brims black. The traffic cop on the corner wore an umpire's mask, his arms held out as he signaled safe, then out, then safe again, then neither, then both. Dock laughed, but the sound curdled in his mouth.

Billboards stacked themselves along the street, more vivid now and more insistent. A Marlboro ad showed the cowboy's face wiped blank, the cigarette burning a hole straight through the skyline. A Warhol print for soup hung crooked beside it, and one can was upside down, leaking color. Dock felt the savory flavor spill onto his tongue. He tasted tin and salt and something else he recognized, something like the inside of a well-worn baseball glove.

At each block the signs grew larger and louder. They multiplied and overlapped until every message fought for space. It became impossible to tell which one was meant for the city and which one had been hung there for him alone.

Horns rose in waves of cheers, then flattened back into traffic. Palm trees bowed and swayed, their fronds chopping the air like an umpire ringing up strike three.

Then the tunnel swallowed them whole.

Darkness pressed in, the cab rocking through its throat. The windshield became a mirror, and Dock saw things blooming in the glass. First, faint outlines: an umpire's mask, hollow-eyed, rising like a moon - its empty eyes stared straight through him as the cab hurtled on. It was a mask of authority, of power, and of the final word - a symbol of the game that stretched endlessly before him.

The stitches bit deeper the more he struggled, tugging his skin toward the vinyl. His arms prickled, hot needles threading into muscle, drawing him tighter and tighter against the seat until he swore he could feel the rhythm of the cab itself pulsing through him. Every beat another knot, every breath a loop cinched.

Something moved in the side window, not a reflection and not light. Fingers. White fingers dragged slow across the glass, nails scraping in a silence that felt worse than any scream. He turned his head but the pane showed only his own face, mouth open and eyes wide. Then the mask lowered over it, bars descending, steel shadows crawling across his reflection until his own eyes disappeared inside the grid.

The cab rocked harder. Dock's stomach rolled. The bulbs in the ceiling popped in sequence, one after another, as if counting him down. Shadows bloomed in the spaces between each burst of light. Long limbs stretched across the roof. Bent arms reached. The Umpire's mask leaned in through the windshield, bars glowing with a sick shine, every unseen breath behind it swelling like a hurricane filling a tunnel.

Dock clawed at the seams on his forearms, his throat pulling tight and dry. He told himself it was the acid. Just the acid. Only the acid. But the air had changed. It had become thick as syrup, too heavy to swallow, too heavy to breathe. He felt that if he opened his mouth wide enough the dark would pour in and drown him from the inside out.

The tires hummed low and steady. The hum bent itself into words. Do not miss the signs. Do not miss the signs. With every repetition, Dock felt the mask lean closer, pulling him down into some place beneath the world, some place without rules or chalk lines or daylight.

Panic hit him like a spark catching dry brush. Every nerve lit at once. He pressed both palms against the glass as if he could push the nightmare out of the cab. The reflection only deepened. The Umpire's mask now filled the entire windshield, bars glowing with their own fever, void eyes locked on him. He heard breath behind it, ragged and enormous, like the tunnel itself had lungs that were expanding to swallow him whole.

And then a shift. A clean, sharp smell cut through the dark. Not gasoline. Not leather. Pine tar. Oiled mitt. Warm hide under stadium lamps.

Manny's mitt.

Dock exhaled hard, lungs catching. Manny crouched behind the plate in his mind, steady as stone, mask tilted, fingers flicking just enough to guide him. Manny Sanguillén was the heartbeat of the Pirates, squatting behind the plate nearly every night, his bat as sharp as his chatter. If Clemente was their legend and Stargell their voice, Manny was the daily pulse that kept the team alive.

Chaos distilled into signals. Manny, the translator. The compass. The only one Dock trusted to keep him true.

In the tunnel glass, for a blink, Manny's mask flared against the Umpire's empty one. Light against dark, tether against abyss. The two images fought for space, overlapped, and flickered like dueling signals on a scoreboard. Dock gripped the seat and whispered Manny's name, and the vision shattered.

Light detonated across the cab. The tunnel tore open. Sun slammed into the windshield, too harsh and too raw to feel real.

The cab surged toward the airport, but Dock was already measuring distance. San Diego. The mound. Manny crouched and waiting. The tether that might keep him from drifting off the world entirely.

Dock squinted, voice barely more than a breath. "Manny. I am gonna need you again today, my man."

CHAPTER THREE

A Disturbance at Thirty Thousand Feet

Overhead, the public address system cracked alive. A woman's voice, flat and official, repeated itself in a loop: *"The white zone is for advancing, the black zone is for removal."* The words bent in Dock's head.

There has to be a different way to say that, he thought.

He scratched the side of his head, shook it once, and kept moving. Around him, travelers tugged their carry-ons, kissed goodbyes at the curb, lined up in orderly queues. No one else seemed to hear it the way he had.

He rubbed his face, not surprised. *The white zone is for loading, the red zone is for unloading.* That's what she must've said. That's what everyone else must've heard. His gut told him otherwise.

At the security counter he slid his ID across the table. The officer studied it a beat longer than Dock liked, thumb pressing the corner, eyes moving from card to face and back again. Nothing was said. No smirk. No jab. Just a pause that stretched too long and made the air feel thin.

The couple ahead of him had breezed through, sure, but maybe this guy was just slow. Maybe thorough. Dock felt his jaw tighten anyway, the acid gnawing at the edges of his patience. He shifted his weight, fighting the urge to shuffle his feet like a guilty man waiting on a verdict.

When the ID finally came back, Dock nodded, tucked it into his pocket, and kept moving.

The flight board overhead flickered, each letter snapping into place with a loud clack. Destinations cycled past in sterile green. Chicago. Dallas. Denver. Dock's eyes tracked the rhythm until his own number finally slid into place. San Diego. On Time. He stared at it until the letters blurred, waiting for some trick of his mind to bend them into something else, but nothing changed. Just San Diego. Just a gate and a boarding call waiting to happen.

He exhaled through his nose, rolled his shoulders once, and let the crowd carry him forward.

The concourse stretched long, lined with chrome and glass. Rows of molded chairs crowded around square ashtrays. The sand inside was dotted with half-buried cigarette butts that still smoldered in little orange breaths. A stewardess in a fitted blue uniform strode past, heels clicking against the tile, her perfume trailing behind her like smoke. Dock caught the scent, sweet and heavy, and let it pass as quickly as it came.

A woman in a green dress struggled with a stroller near the gate, snapping its joints into place while a baby wailed red-faced inside. A man in a gray suit barked into a pay-phone, pacing tight angry circles, the cord wrapped around his wrist like a snare. Farther down, three kids tore into bags of peanuts at a candy stand, laughing so loud it turned heads. Dock let the sounds wash over him. Mundane life. Ordinary life. All of it sharp as pins against the faint buzz that still worked along his nerves.

He checked the wall clock above the counter. Just past nine. He worked the numbers in his head like innings. Three hours to San Diego, another hour to the ballpark. That gave him a cushion, but not much. Five hours until first pitch. No bullpen session. No chance to stretch it out. Just a straight walk onto the mound.

His fingers twitched, gripping at air, working seams that were not there.

The smell of jet fuel seeped in through the sliding doors, threading with the tang of polish and the sweet-stale haze of smoke. Dock adjusted the strap of his bag higher, tightened his jacket across his shoulders, and kept moving.

Ahead, the gate agent waved a family through with a plastic smile. Another traveler slapped his ticket down, barely looking up from his briefcase. The line moved in small ripples, steady and practiced. Dock joined it without a word, ticket pinched between two fingers, eyes fixed on the tunnel ahead.

The terminal doors yawned wide, promising nothing more than departure. Dock lifted his chin, pushed his hands into his pockets, and walked through like a man heading into a start he had not prepared for but would face all the same.

The jetway funneled Dock into the cabin, warm with recycled air and the smell of upholstery. A stewardess in a blue uniform smiled and gestured down the aisle.

"Back of the bus, sir," she said.

Dock froze. "What?"

She blinked, smile never slipping. "Back of the *plane*, sir. Row twenty-two. Enjoy your flight and please let us know if you need anything at all."

He stared at her another beat, heart kicking against his ribs. She didn't flinch. She even seemed comforting. Just another day, another passenger to seat. Dock muttered thanks and moved on, but the words lingered. Back of the bus. Maybe he'd misheard. Maybe he hadn't. Dock dismissed it along with the paranoia that defined his entire morning since the phone call.

The rows stretched narrow, shoulders brushing as people stowed coats and briefcases. Dock slid into his seat, pressed his bag under the chair ahead, and leaned back. The vinyl squeaked under him, sharp and clean. For the first time since morning, his pulse slowed. The hum in his blood began to thin. Maybe the acid was burning off. Maybe he'd settle before first pitch.

He let his shoulders sink into the seat, the vinyl cool against his back. The steady rumble of the engines was no menace now, only background, the same low murmur a ballpark crowd makes before the anthem. His breath evened out. His hands unclenched. For the first time all day he felt less like a man being chased and more like a man on his way to work.

Dock closed his eyes and pictured the mound, the give of the dirt under his cleats, Manny crouched low with his glove open like a target. That image steadied him. He almost believed the morning had been nothing but nerves, nothing but a bad start to a long day.

The engines droned low as the plane taxied. Through the oval window, the tarmac blurred by. Dock closed his eyes, letting the vibration settle him, rocking like a dugout bench on game day. For a few blessed minutes, it all felt normal.

At cruising altitude, the cart rolled past, the clink of bottles and the rustle of paper cups. Dock shook his head at the stewardess's offer, rose instead, and edged down the aisle toward the lavatory.

The bathroom was narrow, barely big enough for him to turn. Fluorescent light buzzed overhead, steady and white. Dock splashed water on his face, rubbed it over his cheeks, and pulled his shaving kit from the small pouch he carried. The blade whispered across his skin, clean and ordinary. Each stroke should have felt jagged, each scrape like scales tearing loose, but it did not. Smooth. Controlled. For the first time that day he thought maybe he was in the clear.

Then the lights flickered.

Just a pulse at first, dim then bright. He steadied his hand on the sink and waited for it to pass. But the hum shifted. It bent into a low guttural moan, like engines straining in reverse.

The plane jolted. Dock lurched sideways, shoulder slamming into the wall. Another jolt hit, harder this time. His razor clattered to the floor. The sink rattled against the tile, water spraying from the faucet as if the whole room had come loose from the fuselage.

Then the floor dropped away from him.

He was weightless. His body pitched upward and slammed into the ceiling hard enough to rattle his teeth. His skull struck the panel above with a dull thud that left his vision swimming with sparks. The walls twisted around him. Angles bent where they had no right to bend. Seams split like fabric tearing under strain.

Dock clawed for balance, nails scraping plastic that felt too warm. His tie whipped forward and snapped taut, caught in the toilet's suction. The bowl gaped wider and wider, no longer porcelain but a black mouth, a drain that led nowhere, pulling at him with steady hunger.

He braced his legs against the wall and yanked at the silk as the roar grew louder. Engines, wind, void, all of it blended into one sound, a storm trying to drag him down the hole. The pull sucked the air from his lungs, his skin tugging toward the spiral. His hands slipped on porcelain slick with condensation.

His knees slammed the floor. A bolt of pain shot up his thigh. He grunted, breath torn from him as the pressure shoved him sideways again. His shoulder cracked against the mirror, spiderwebbing glass across his reflection. For a moment he saw himself split a dozen times, each Dock wide-eyed, mouth open in a scream he couldn't hear.

The room lurched and spun. The floor tilted vertical, pitching him sideways. He tumbled, arms smacking walls, hip bruising hard on the sink. His cheek split against the corner. He tasted copper, thick and hot.

The tie dragged again, jerking his neck forward, choking him. He tore at it, pulling until threads burned his palms raw. The knot held. His windpipe shrank to a straw. Spots filled his vision, black edging out the light.

The sink gushed water like a broken hydrant, pressure blasting until it stung his skin. The overhead bulb stuttered, flaring bright and then dropping him into darkness. In the shadows the seams of the walls peeled back further, plastic panels bowing outward as if the cabin itself were alive and ready to split him into the sky.

Dock kicked at the toilet, his foot slamming porcelain until pain flared sharp in his ankle. He gasped, a thin rasp of air forcing itself into his lungs. Threads along his tie began to snap one by one with tiny pops. Each break felt like a fiber of him giving way.

The ceiling buckled next. It bowed toward him, seams cracking with a scream that sounded like metal tearing itself in half. The roar climbed into a pitch so high it drilled straight through his skull. He felt warm wetness at his ear and knew it was blood. He slammed both palms against the sink, teeth clenched hard enough to ache, convinced the entire plane had dropped into a dive.

For a split second he thought he was going through the opening. He imagined himself sucked into nothing, scattered across the sky, his body ripped apart before he could even draw breath to scream.

Then the roar cut off.

The tie went slack. His shoes hit the floor with a thud. Light blinked steady, monotonous hum returning, flat and harmless. The sink gurgled, water running clear. The mirror was whole, no cracks, no split faces staring back.

Dock staggered back, chest heaving, ribs aching. His lip was split, shoulder throbbing where it had met the wall, and a welt already swelling above his brow. He pressed one hand to the glass, fingers trembling, half expecting it to ripple under his touch.

The shaving kit lay scattered across the tile, brush and blade skittered to the corners. He bent to gather them, hands shaking, breath scraping raw through his throat. Blood dripped from his nose, smearing across the handle of the razor.

When he opened the door, the aisle was calm. Passengers reclined in their seats, heads against cushions, papers folded in laps. A child giggled at a comic book. A woman sipped her drink, ice clicking in the glass. No one looked up.

Dock blinked, dizzy. His shirt clung damp against his back, sweat soaking through. His tie hung in shreds, frayed ends swinging against his chest. He shoved it into his jacket, smearing another streak of blood across the fabric.

A stewardess passed, steady on her feet, tray balanced easily. "Please take your seat, sir. We'll be landing shortly."

Her voice was calm, almost kind. No urgency, no sign of turbulence. Dock stared at her, throat raw, but managed a nod.

He moved back toward his row in a daze, shoes heavy on the carpet. Each step sent a shiver through his battered body, pain layered into every joint. He lowered himself into his seat, pressed his palms flat against his knees, and stared at the window.

Outside, clouds slid past, white and serene, as if the sky had never held anything but peace.

The cabin hummed like nothing had happened.

The taxi ride gave him quiet. No jolts. No sudden voices bending sideways. Only the hum of tires on asphalt and the steady blink of stoplights. Dock leaned back, cheek pressed to the glass, letting the city roll by in fragments. Palm trees blurred into neon signs. A boy pedaled a rusted Schwinn along the curb as if trying to outrun the afternoon.

His chest still ached from the flight, ribs sore where the walls had slammed him. He touched the welt above his brow and winced. The cut at his lip had dried, the copper taste gone, but the sting remained. That was what gnawed at him. If nothing had happened, if it was only in his head, why did his body feel beaten?

Maybe the acid had not burned off after all. Maybe reality itself was folding and unfolding and he was just along for the ride.

The cab turned and the stadium rose into view.

San Diego Stadium sat in the valley like a concrete colossus. Three years old and already proud, its light towers stood rigid against the sky, pale blue beams glinting under the sun. Half the lower bowl was permanent concrete, the other half modular seating that could be rolled out, retracted, reshaped depending on the sport. To Dock's eye the sections looked like ribs of some sleeping animal, flexing under its own weight.

As the cab drew closer the lines of the building warped in his vision. Sections opened and closed again. Angles shifted. For a moment the place seemed to breathe. It was as if the stadium were alive and deciding what kind of game would be played today between the Padres and the visiting Pirates.

The outfield wall stood high, nineteen feet of steel and concrete, too high and too heavy. It was not a wall for baseball. It was a fortress wall. A wall meant to keep something out. Or to keep something in. Dock wondered who was strong enough to muscle a ball over it and almost smiled.

The giant rolling doors cut into the sides gaped like mouths. Some closed, some ajar, as if the stadium itself could choose to swallow or spit out whoever stepped through. But that's baseball. A game where even the greatest hitters are only successful thirty percent of the time.

Dock sat forward, eyes narrowed. No glow, no monstrous movement. Just architecture. Just steel, bolts, and concrete. But it felt too fortified, too watchful, like an arena built for nothing but sport.

The cab rolled to the curb. Dock paid, stepped onto the pavement, and adjusted his jacket against the breeze. The air smelled faintly of cut grass and hot asphalt, the blend of a ballpark on game day in sunny San Diego.

He stood still, staring at the structure that loomed over him. His pulse ticked hard, but the panic from the flight was gone. This was the field. This was his work.

Dock squared himself away, the stadium shadow falling over him like a challenge.

"Alright, daddy," he muttered, voice low but certain. "Let's see if I can still throw."

Chapter Four

Where Stone Meets Storm

Danny Murtaugh perched on the dugout step like a man built for perches, like a gargoyle on a skyscraper. The wad of tobacco bulged his lip, unchewed, as if working it might commit him to a thought he didn't need to have. He ran his eyes over the field, then the sky, then Dock, then the lineup card in his hand. The eyes made notes the mouth didn't.

"Skip," Dock said, voice carrying more swagger than balance.

Murtaugh finally turned, slow as a man checking a storm on the horizon. "You're late."

Dock shrugged. "I'm here."

"You're here now." Murtaugh spat brown into the dirt. "I've already worn a groove in this concrete. Thought I'd have to scratch you, call Moose or Veale on short notice. You think I like scrambling at the last goddamn minute?"

Dock rubbed the ball in his hand like a coin, eyes wide, grin crooked. Then the grin faltered.
"Skip... I don't know how much I got tonight. Don't feel right."

Murtaugh spat again, eyes narrowing. "You don't get the luxury of not feelin' right, Ellis. We got two today. If you give me five and run for cover, the bullpen's cooked for game two. I need more than that."

Dock shrugged, shoulders loose but voice low. "I'll try."

"Don't try," Murtaugh snapped. He shifted the plug of tobacco with his tongue but kept it set. "You dig in and you pitch. Give me innings, however ugly. Save the damn arms. That's the job tonight. You shut these bums out a week ago your damn self. Do it again, will ya?"

He fixed Dock with a long, gray look. "You pitch tonight because you're on the card, Ellis. Not because I trust you. Don't make me a fool for keeping you there."

Dock smirked, but the smirk wavered at the edges.

A captain navigating weather, not explaining it. Dock had seen the same look on fishermen in Puerto Rico and bus drivers in Pittsburgh—men who knew you don't fix storms; you just pencil the schedule and ride when it comes.

Murtaugh didn't try to fix Dock. He penciled him in, same as rain on the schedule.

Farther down the bench, trainer Tony Bartirome kneeled with a spool of tape between his fingers, wrapping a rookie's wrist in clean spirals. His knuckles were nicked and shiny with ointment, the hands of a man who'd patched more miles than he'd ever run. A pot of liniment stood open like a brass chalice, the sharp wintergreen cutting even through the tobacco and smoke. Bartirome's hands moved with a small, practiced cadence—pull, smooth, tear. The rhythm was so steady it might've been a marching beat.

He didn't look at Dock until the knot cinched. Then his eyes did the thing Murtaugh's had: a measure, a recognition, like a mechanic listening to an engine he already knows is misfiring.

"You want heat, I got heat," Bartirome said, palm hovering over the jar. "Want cold, I got cold. Want peace, you're on your own."

"Just the arm," Dock said. His voice was thin on the last word.

Bartirome nodded, dipped two fingers into the liniment, and began to rub wintergreen into Dock's forearm with the same churchly care he'd just given the rookie's wrist. The burn rose sharp and clean, like peppermint fire. Dock closed his eyes, let the sting distract him. For a moment the ball in his hand felt less like a weight and more like a tool.

"Bodies tell on themselves," Bartirome said lightly, as if he were only filling the silence. His thumbs pressed circles into Dock's tendons, drawing heat down toward the wrist. "Minds, now... minds keep secrets. The tricky ones."

The ointment sank into Dock's skin, a burning thread weaving through muscle and sinew, stitching the space between nerves. The scent filled his nostrils—sharp, biting, alive—and he felt it crawl along his forearm, an invasion of warmth that unfurled like smoke in the air. Each press of Bartirome's thumbs sent ripples deeper, flooding the channels of his arm with a strange heat that pulsed against his bones.

Dock kept his eyes closed, but behind his lids, colors flickered. The vibrant green of the liniment mingled with swirling patterns that felt like they were made from the very fabric of the universe—cosmic stitching that threaded through the fabric of time and space. He imagined the ointment seeping into the marrow of his bones, pulling him further down into the earth, anchoring him to some hidden truth just below the surface. The heat felt like a promise—a way to bind him to this moment, to the game waiting beyond the dugout.

He clenched his jaw against the rising intensity, caught between the sting of the ointment and the vibrant echoes of the crowd beyond the field. Sounds bled into one another—the crack of a bat, the roar of a fan, the whisper of grass brushing against itself—and he could feel them pooling in his chest, expanding like an ocean ready to spill over. The world outside felt infinite, yet this moment was all-consuming, wrapping around him like a tight cocoon.

"Just the arm," he had said, but it felt like more than that. It felt like the strumming of a guitar against the fibers of his flesh.

"That a doctor's opinion?" Dock muttered, masking the overwhelming sensations.

"That's a janitor's," Bartirome said, and gave the arm a final squeeze before moving on.

Dock flexed his fingers. The arm felt awake, almost humming, but the rest of him still tilted sideways. Bartirome could patch the body. Dock's fracture was elsewhere, the kind no trainer reached. And Bartirome knew it—his glance lingered just a beat too long, as if asking a question he already knew better than to voice.

Roberto Clemente stood at the far end of the dugout, not leaning, not slouching, but standing the way a lion paces inside lines only he can see. The crisp whites sharpened him, the black and gold trim cutting like an edge, and the bat he rested upright was less a tool than a scepter. Men gave him space without realizing they were doing it; even laughter went low when it carried past him.

Dock watched the stillness, the carved angles of jaw and cheek that made Clemente look like someone had sculpted him out of consequence itself. Clemente carried himself as though baseball were beneath him, and yet played as though it were scripture. There was a tension in that dignity — not aloofness, but a weight. He spoke for the voiceless in press rooms, called out slights others swallowed, demanded re-spect not just for himself but for anyone who shared his skin or his tongue. He carried Puerto Rico on his back the way some men carried bats: something to swing, something to shield.

Dock shifted on the bench, ball rolling in his palm, aware that his own code was looser, more jagged, like a hymn hummed off-key. He admired Clemente's gravity, but it weighed on him too — the reminder that some storms never form into order, that not every man born into the game could walk with scripture in his stance. Dock felt like a fault-line shifting under pressure, rumbling without release, while Clemente was the mountain that refused to move.

A booming laugh crashed through the smoke and con-crete, and suddenly the air bent warm. Willie Stargell strode in, shoulders like cathedral doors, a mass of humanity, a body so wide it felt like it held the team inside it. He passed out sunflower seeds as though they were communion wafers, telling a story Dock didn't catch but didn't need to — the rhythm was enough. Stargell's voice filled the dugout like a hearth's glow, a promise that no night game could run too cold.

But Stargell wasn't just warmth. He was thunder given shape, the bat everyone in the stadium knew could change the night with a single swing. Already an All-Star many times over, already the Pirates' most feared hitter, he was the kind of presence pitchers studied like scripture and still couldn't solve. Opposing teams pitched around him, whispered his name like a warning. Teammates leaned toward him as if some of his light might rub off, the way men draw close to a fire when the air goes black.

Dock cracked a grin at the sound but knew it wasn't the same kind of fire. Where Dock crackled with storm, Stargell glowed with hearth. One burned hot and violent, the other gave heat men leaned into. Teammates looked toward Stargell and saw a center of gravity. They looked toward Dock and saw lightning in a bottle — useful, dangerous, maybe about to burst. Stargell's greatness steadied them. Dock's volatility unsettled them. And Dock knew it.

In Dock's head, a voice chattered bright and fast: *Bueno, Dock, bueno… ahora afuera, ahora adentro, give me your smoke.* He turned, expecting Manny Sanguillén's grin, the jittery dance of his feet, the mitt always tapping in rhythm. Manny was noise that doubled as comfort, a fence of words and motion that kept Dock's storm from spilling over.

But the dugout corner was empty. The chatter existed only in memory, bouncing back at Dock like echoes in a cave. He frowned, rolled the ball harder in his palm until the stitches bit. Most days Dock's storm blew into Manny's mitt. Manny's chatter was the fence that kept it from spilling.

Instead Dock felt the tilt again, the same off-kilter sway he'd carried since stepping into the park. Clemente's dignity, Stargell's warmth, Manny's chatter — three kinds of order. Dock had none of them. He was something else entirely, something unmoored, pacing like a storm without boundaries.

The lineup card hung under greasy glass near the trainer's table, typed in neat black letters. It was ritual more than record — every man on the team eventually drifted by, eyes skimming down as if reading their own fate.

Dock stepped up, ball rolling in his palm, eyes following the order slot by slot.

Alou, CF. Matty, quick as a shadow, first step like a thief. A man who carved doubles out of groundballs, always moving, always poking at daylight.

Alley, SS. Gene, thin and stubborn, a glove sharper than his bat. The kind of man who held the middle together, quiet as mortar.

Clemente, RF. Gravity in human form, carved angles, the lion who carried an island on his back. Dock's chest tightened just seeing the name, as if consequence itself had been typed in black ink.

Robertson, 3B. Bob, strong-armed, square-shouldered, hot and cold as a furnace with a bad draft. On his good nights he could open the clouds; on bad ones he was a shadow.

Stargell, LF. Willie, the fire in the hearth, the bat that could end arguments with a single swing. His name glowed even in plain type — a presence larger than the dugout walls.

Dock's eyes dropped to the next line.

May, C.

The floor tilted half a degree. Dock felt his cleats scrape against the concrete just to keep balance, the sound unnaturally sharp in his ears, like a nail dragged down a chalkboard no one else seemed to hear. He blinked once, then again, waiting for the letters to unstick, to loosen, to fall back into the familiar rhythm of *Sanguillén.*

For a heartbeat, the black ink quivered. He swore he saw it curl into Manny's loops, heard the chatter that usually fenced him in — the machine-gun Spanish spilling behind his ear, the mitt snapping like a gate: *Bueno, Dock... ahora afuera, ahora adentro. Give me your smoke.* Dock's shoulders twitched as if to answer. He even tasted the cab ride in the back of his throat, that moment when the tunnel walls had breathed and he'd seen a catcher's mask hovering there — Manny's mask, distorted but steady, the one thing that had cut through the hum of neon and prophecy.

But the vision snapped.

The name held fast. Stubborn, black, immovable: **May.**

Dock pressed his thumb so hard into the seams of the ball that the stitches bit, as if he could drag himself back to balance through touch alone. He needed Manny tonight.

Needed the chatter, the constant fence of words, the noise that kept the storm inside him from spilling over.

Instead he got Jerry.

Jerry May, silent as a stone. Not Manny's energy, not his rhythm. But Jerry had been there at the beginning — Dock's first game, his first breath in the big leagues. The memory flickered like an old reel: Jerry crouched low, steady mitt, calling pitches without flourish. A different kind of anchor. Not the fence, but the post it tied to.

Dock's throat dried. The thought tilted him again: maybe fate had circled back to its starting point. Maybe it was Jerry's mitt, not Manny's, that was meant to catch this game.

"Guess it's you after all, Jerry," Dock muttered.

From behind him, Jerry May's voice came steady as stone. "That's right. You got me."

Dock turned. Jerry was lacing his gear with calm hands, no chatter, no grin, just quiet efficiency. Where Manny was motion and noise, Jerry was stillness. A fence built not of noise but of posts sunk deep.

Dock knew it wasn't unusual. Catchers were swapped, rotated, spelled like tires. But the knowledge didn't soothe. Most nights his storm blew into Manny's mitt. Manny's chatter was the fence that kept it from spilling. Tonight that fence was gone.

Oliver, 1B. Dock's eyes slid lower, needing the rest of the lineup like a rope line in the dark. Young Al, steady bat, quick smile — still new, still green, but solid wood.

Mazeroski, 2B. Bill, the man of 1960, wrists made of flint, glove that chewed up grounders. The name itself a monument.

And last, the card returned Dock's gaze in plain type:

Ellis, P.

His own name looked foreign there, like someone else's appointment he was keeping.

Jerry May stood, chest protector hanging loose, mitt already pounding once, twice, in a rhythm as steady as a metronome. "One sign if we're rolling," he said. "Two if we're fishing. You don't like something, you shake it like you mean it."

Dock nodded, though his throat felt dry.

Most nights belonged to Manny. But not this one. This one belonged to Jerry May.

After the lineup card, the clubhouse noise drained to a hush. The chatter that had filled the dugout — Stargell's laugh, Clemente's clipped phrases, the scratch of tape and the murmur of trainers — all thinned into background hum. The air felt heavier, as though the room had inhaled but chosen not to exhale.

In that quiet, Dock saw him.

Don Osborn sat in the shadows near the bat rack, cap pulled low, arms folded across his chest. For a moment Dock thought he was looking at a piece of the dugout itself — a post, a fixture, something built into the concrete. Only when the eyes lifted did the figure become flesh.

They weren't sharp eyes. They were steady eyes, flat and patient, like stones worn smooth by a river.

Osborn had nearly two hundred wins in towns most fans had never heard of. Long bus rides, splintered clubhouses, pitching mounds that were more dirt clod than clay. They'd called him *The Wizard of Oz* in the minors, a name half-mocking, half-reverent. Magic enough to win, never enough to be called up. He never touched a major-league mound, never once let his name ring in a stadium as bright as this fortress by the sea. His career was rumor turned caretaker, and now he watched over the men who did make it.

He didn't bark orders. He didn't puff himself up with wisdom. He watched.

Dock shifted under that gaze.

Osborn didn't look at him like Murtaugh did — tallying him up as a problem to manage, an inning to be stretched, an arm to be rationed. He didn't look like Bartirome either — recognizing a fracture that tape couldn't reach. Osborn's eyes carried something slower, heavier. He looked at Dock the way a mason studies a crack in a wall he built long ago, patient but unblinking, measuring how far it's spread, knowing it won't close again on its own.

Dock rolled the ball in his palm, restless. Osborn didn't move.

The dugout felt like a stage where two figures had taken their marks — one jittering with fire, the other solid as stone. Dock's breath came fast, shallow, as if he were already on the mound. Osborn's chest barely rose.

For a moment Dock felt time stretch, a camera panning from his own wide eyes to Osborn's half-hidden stare. Two elements, bound to clash.

One man carried the elements in his blood. The other was stone. And even stone erodes.

A drip from the ceiling found a crack in the concrete and spread into a dark vein across the floor, inching toward the bench. Dock watched it with a kind of awe, as if the earth itself had decided to leak beneath them. He looked back at Osborn and saw the man's gaze fixed on the same creeping waterline.

Neither spoke. Neither needed to.

Don Osborn remained in the shadows, steady and silent, the rock. But he knew, as all rocks do — water always wins.

CHAPTER FIVE

Through the Bullpen Glass

Heat shimmered off the infield like a curtain of clear water. Dock stepped from the dugout and felt the world tighten. The chalk lines pulsed faintly under the sun, not moving enough to name, just breathing slow as a sleeping animal.

He tipped his cap and found Jerry May already crouched behind the plate. Jerry looked like stone carved into the shape of a man. The way he set up, the way he breathed; every movement was economy. Dock rolled the ball between his palms. The seams were warm. They shouldn't have been.

"Warm enough for you?" Jerry called, voice clipped, practical.

"Feels like the whole world's a stove," Dock said.

Jerry smiled through the mask. "Then the ball will fly."

Dock nodded. "You seeing it? That shimmer?"

"Just heat," Jerry said. "Don't chase ghosts before the anthem's cold."

He crouched again and flashed a sign. One finger. Then two. Then there was something else, a shape Dock couldn't name. A spiral. Then gone. Jerry didn't flinch.

Dock set, threw. The ball vanished. Then reappeared in Jerry's glove, smoke whispering off the pocket.

Jerry blinked, looked at the glove, then back at Dock. "You put something on that?"

"No," Dock said, rubbing his fingers. "You see it disappear?"

"Ball came through fine."

"You're telling me you didn't?"

"I caught it, didn't I?" Jerry stood, tossed it back. "You're just wound up."

Dock caught it bare-handed and felt it hum. "It's alive, man."

"Then throw it before it dies." Jerry crouched again. "Let's see if you can find the zone this time."

Dock wound, released. Pop. The glove echoed deep, hollow. Jerry held it there a second too long.

"You're behind your hand," he said. "Get on top."

"I'm trying," Dock said, breathing through his teeth. "Feels like the mound's breathing back."

Jerry gave him a look through the bars. "It's dirt, Dock. Dirt doesn't breathe."

"You ever listen close enough?"

"I listen to pitchers," Jerry said. "Not dirt."

Dock stepped off, wiped his palm on his thigh, looked around the field. Clemente was a statue in right. Stargell flicked shells into the grass. The rest of the team looked fixed in a single moment, like a photograph waiting to be developed.

Jerry walked halfway to the mound. "You want to talk about it or throw through it?"

"Can't talk if the air's melting," Dock muttered.

Jerry frowned. "Then don't breathe it. Just throw."

Dock grinned. "That's your solution for everything, huh?"

"Only the problems that start sixty feet six inches away."

He tossed the ball back. Dock felt the weight, heavier now, like the seams had soaked up blood. He gripped it tighter.

"You're thinking too loud," Jerry said.

"What?"

"I can hear you thinking from here. Quiet your head."

"You ever trip, Jerry?"

Jerry tilted his head. "Trip?"

"Not your feet. Your mind."

"No," Jerry said. "I like knowing what ground looks like."

"Yeah. You would." Dock looked down at the circle around his feet. "I don't think this ground's what it used to be."

Jerry adjusted his crouch. "You've been saying that since spring training."

"Not like this."

"Every mound feels cursed when your arm's tight."

Dock rolled the ball between his palms, eyes on the dirt. The bullpen clay was packed darker than the field, rich as wet blood. He pressed his spike down and watched the indent hold its shape too long. "This one's breathing."

Jerry lifted the mask. "You breathing too?"

Dock grinned. "Trying to."

"Then we're good."

Jerry settled again, glove open. "Let's get two more. I'll call it."

Dock nodded, wound, threw. The ball cut through the late-afternoon light and hit the mitt with a dull, hollow pop that echoed against the concrete wall behind them. Jerry didn't flinch. He lobbed it back with one smooth motion.

Dock caught it barehanded and hissed. The leather pulsed once in his grip, a faint heartbeat that belonged to neither of them.

"You feel that?" Dock asked.

"Feel what?"

"The ball. It's... it's humming."

Jerry snorted. "Then it's ready for the show."

He crouched again, raised two fingers. Dock squinted. The digits flickered, blurred, became something else entirely. They became a twist of shape, a symbol drawn in the air that burned for half a second, then was gone.

"What was that?" Dock asked.

"What was what?" Jerry called back, steady as ever. "Two fingers. You've seen it before."

"Didn't look like fingers to me."

"Then stop staring at them."

Dock breathed out through his nose, tried to laugh. "You ever trip, Jerry?"

"On what, the grass?"

"No," Dock said. "On yourself."

Jerry tapped his mask with one finger. "I've seen enough without chemical help."

Dock stared past him, through the chain link, to the field. The sunlight had shifted. The air was still. Somewhere, a gull hung motionless above left field, wings out, suspended. The hum of the crowd beyond the wall merged into one sustained note, low and endless. It vibrated through the bullpen fence, through his shoes, through the ball in his hand.

He threw again.

The pitch carried a thin streak of light that only he could see. When it struck Jerry's mitt, a breath of smoke curled upward. Jerry waved it away.

"Arm's live," Jerry said. "You're ready."

Dock wiped his mouth with the back of his hand. "That didn't look right."

"It looked fine from where I'm sitting."

"You didn't see the smoke?"

"You ever think maybe you're just running hot?" Jerry said, voice light but not joking. "You're always running hot."

Dock looked at him. Jerry's mask caught the sun at a strange angle, and for a second the bars seemed to multiply. The face behind it blurred, split, then resolved again.

"Hey," Jerry said. "Eyes up. Skip's waving."

Murtaugh's voice drifted over the outfield grass, thin but sharp: "That's enough. Bring him in."

Dock turned. The bullpen gate was open. Beyond it, the field shimmered white in the sun, every blade of grass twitching in the heat. He could see the dugout through the mirage, but it looked far away, distorted, as if stretched down a long hallway that hadn't existed before.

Jerry stood, tossed him the ball. "Go get it."

Dock caught it against his chest. The seams burned faintly through his shirt. "You coming?"

"I'll see you out there," Jerry said.

The sunlight flickered again across his mask, and for a moment it wasn't Jerry at all, only the hollow outline of a catcher's gear with no face inside.

Dock blinked. Jerry was there again, smiling small, glove slung under one arm.

"Go on," Jerry said. "You're burning daylight."

Dock turned toward the gate. The hum in the air rose, low and steady, the same note that had haunted every breath since Los Angeles. The field beyond the fence rippled, beckoning. He touched the gate, felt it tremble like something alive, and stepped through.

CHAPTER SIX

Under the Mask, Something Listened

The game began in sunlight too clean to trust. It was the kind of light that flattens the world until everything looks repainted for television. The Pirates took the field in visiting gray, black caps low, the gold P gleaming like something newly minted.

Dock sat half-hidden in the dugout, elbows on his knees, cap pulled down. The air tasted metallic, like the inside of a transistor radio. Beyond the rail, the field shimmered. The crowd was one great, breathing animal, swaying in heat and color.

At home plate, the Umpire adjusted his mask. For a moment Dock thought the man glanced straight at him, though Dock hadn't even moved.

Then the first pitch of the night cut through the air.

"Strrrrike one."

The call did not echo. It did not carry. It simply arrived inside Dock's skull, clear and direct, without air between thought and sound. His teammates heard nothing strange. They leaned and watched and spat into the dust.

Another pitch.

"Strike two," the Umpire said, too sing-song, too pleased. He stretched the vowel, and somewhere inside that stretched sound Dock thought he heard a giggle.

Clemente was up. First at-bat. The swing came quick, the contact real, a foul ball straight back, vanishing into the stands.

But the Umpire did not move. He turned his head toward the visitors' dugout and pointed.

Straight at Dock.

"Strike three," he sang, voice rising in pitch, almost cheerful.

Clemente stood still for a moment, bat hanging loose. Then he stepped away from the box, muttering under his breath, "Dos strikes, not three."

The inning went on, baseball pretending nothing had happened. But Dock could not stop watching the Umpire. The man stood too still, too straight, as if something else were holding him upright.

When the Pirates came in empty-handed, Dock followed them through the half-lit tunnel that led to the field. His cleats clicked against the concrete, each step echoing twice, one real, one delayed, as if time itself were deciding whether to move forward.

Bottom of the first

The sun had sunk low, throwing orange light through the steel ribs of the stadium. Dock walked to the mound, rolling the ball in his palm. It throbbed faintly, a living pulse against his skin.

He glanced toward home. The Umpire waited, crouched, mask gleaming like polished obsidian.

Dock came set. First pitch, high. Ball one. Second, wide again. Ball two.

The Umpire's hand stayed lazy at his side.

From the dugout, Murtaugh's voice carried. "Find it, Ellis. Let them hit it."

Dock exhaled through his nose. "Working on it."

The next pitch split the plate. He knew it. Everyone knew it.

"Ball three," the Umpire called, bright as a bell.

Dock smirked. "Guess we're playing by feel tonight."

Fourth pitch, too high, too fast. Walk.

The batter trotted to first. The seams dug half-moons into Dock's fingers. The Umpire hummed softly behind the mask, a tune Dock could not place, something halfway between a hymn and a child's rhyme.

Another hitter. Another walk. Two men on, none out.

Jerry May jogged to the mound, mask dangling from his hand. "You good?"

"Yeah," Dock said, jaw tight. "You hear him humming?"

"Humming who?"

Dock shook it off. "Never mind."

May crouched again. Dock threw. The bunt came soft, off the bat's tip. Dock charged, scooped, fired to Mazeroski covering. Out. The runners advanced, second and third.

The next batter dug in. Dock worked him to a full count. The air thickened.

He threw, the ball tailing late, high. The crack sounded pure and awful.

It rose toward deep right.

The next batter dug in. Dock worked him to a full count, his breath coming shorter each pitch. The air around the mound seemed to swell, thick with heat and crowd noise that no longer sounded like voices but like wind caught in a bottle.

He reared back and threw. The ball sailed late and high, tailing over the inner half. The crack that followed was pure, merciless.

It rose toward deep right.

Clemente broke on contact. He did not sprint so much as glide, his first step already where the ball was headed. The sunlight hit his shoulders and flashed, a coin tossed into orbit. Dock tracked the white arc, watching it hang longer than physics allowed, waiting for gravity to remember its job.

At the warning track, Clemente extended his glove, palm open, stride never breaking. The ball met leather with a thud that echoed through the park like a door slamming shut.

Second out.

The runner at third hesitated, then lunged for home. Dock saw the blur of legs, the flash of white uniform, the cloud of dust beginning to rise.

Clemente's body was already turning. One pivot, smooth as clockwork. His left foot planted, the right swept through, and the throw exploded from his hand as if pulled by something more precise than muscle.

The ball carried no arc. It was a line of gold cutting through the field, spinning so hard the seams glowed red. It crossed the diamond faster than sound, a perfect thread connecting right field to the plate.

Jerry May caught it on the fly, chest-high, glove snapping shut like the jaws of a trap. He swung the tag across the sliding runner's shoulder in one motion, dust pluming around them.

Out. Third out.

For half a second, everything stilled — no cheer, no movement, just the echo of that throw zipping across the field. Then the crowd erupted, a wall of sound breaking over the infield.

Dock stood frozen, watching Clemente jog back in from right. The man didn't pump his fist or look to the stands. He just walked, calm, head down, the sunlight following him like obedience.

Dock lifted his glove toward him in salute. Clemente didn't look up. He simply adjusted his cap and kept walking, the crowd still chanting his name.

For the first time all night, Dock felt something true. Not faith or luck, but geometry — an invisible rule drawn perfectly through chaos. For a moment, the world had lines again, clean and straight, as if Clemente's throw had stitched the field back together.

Then the sound inside Dock's head returned. A quiet voice, familiar and amused.
"Beautiful arm," it whispered. "Shame about the man it saves."

Dock froze halfway to the dugout. He looked back. The Umpire had not moved. Mask gleaming. Hands resting easy at his sides.

May nudged him. "Come on, man. Inning's over."

Dock followed, but the voice followed too, threading between the cheers, whispering just loud enough to stay remembered.

Top of the second

The Pirates came up quiet, still buzzing from Clemente's throw. Dave Roberts worked quick on the mound, a rhythm Dock recognized from the dugout. Roberts was one of those pitchers who needed motion to stay calm. Slow meant thinking, and thinking meant doubt. His glove snapped against his thigh between pitches, a nervous tick that beat like a second heart. Alou grounded out on a sharp one-hopper to third. Alley lifted a lazy fly to short left. Two gone in a blur.

Stargell stepped from the on-deck circle and the noise shifted. It was not louder, only heavier, the crowd's breath catching as one. Roberts tugged at his cap and looked anywhere but the plate. He had faced Stargell before. Everyone in the league had. There were stories that still circled the minors about balls he had hit that never came down.

Willie dug in, one slow practice swing tracing an invisible arc over his shoulder. He felt the weight of the lumber settle into his hands. The world narrowed to the small space between him and the mound. That was the part he understood best: two men and one truth, the kind that could only be proven once the ball left the hand.

Roberts nodded to his catcher. The first pitch came up and in, a little message. Willie leaned back just enough, lips tightening. He did not bother to look at the mound. Pitchers liked to think they could rattle you. The trick was to make them realize you did not need to talk to win a conversation.

The second pitch came faster, over the outside corner. Roberts was trying to stretch the zone, see if he would chase. Stargell's eyes tracked the spin, perfect, patient. Strike one, said the umpire. Willie breathed out through his nose. "You found the edge," he murmured, "but not the line."

Roberts stepped off, scuffed the dirt with his heel. He wanted to believe he had room to work. The third sign came, and he shook it off. Too much pride to waste a fastball on a man like Stargell. He chose the curve. He wanted to show he could bend something beautiful and still make it break.

The ball left his hand and hung for a blink longer than it should have. Willie saw it the way some men see their reflection in water, everything distorted but true at its core. The pitch was dying right where he wanted it. He uncoiled from the hips, a single, fluent motion that turned muscle into thunder.

The sound did not only echo, but expanded. A deep crack that rolled through the park and sent heads snapping upward. Roberts knew it was gone before he finished his follow-through. He dropped his glove to his thigh and whispered something that might have been a prayer. The catcher stayed crouched, watching the ball rise into the white light until it disappeared.

Willie started his trot. First base, second, third, each step deliberate. He did not rush. The moment belonged to him, but he let the crowd have it. A father in the stands lifted his son onto his shoulders. Reporters at the press box scribbled notes they would rewrite later to make the swing sound human. From the dugout, Dock leaned forward, grinning despite himself.

When Stargell touched home, Murtaugh clapped once. Not a cheer, a confirmation. "That's how you answer," he said quietly.

The scoreboard flipped to 1–0, the numbers bright against the fading day. The Pirates clapped, the Padres exhaled. Roberts walked to the back of the mound, staring into the dirt as if it could explain what he had done wrong.

For a breath, the game was only baseball again. No strange light, no whispers, only the clean perfection of cause and effect. Stargell sat, unwrapping a stick of gum, and said to no one, "You hang it, I'll bang it." A simple truth spoken into air that, for the moment, still belonged to men.

Between innings

Bartirome crouched beside Dock, rubbing liniment into his shoulder. The wintergreen burned through the fabric of his undershirt, sharp and alive.

"Paper rights don't fit the sidewalk," a voice murmured against Dock's skull.

He flinched. "What?"

Tony glanced up. "Said, you better fight to keep your stride strong. You're tightening up, Ellis."

Dock nodded too quickly. "Right. Thought you said something else."

Tony chuckled, rubbing deeper. "You're hearing things, man. Stretch it out."

Dock did, but the rhythm of the two phrases overlapped in his mind. *Paper rights, better fight. Sidewalk, stride strong.* For a moment, he could not tell which world he had heard them in. The Los Angeles blue and the San Diego blue may have been different shades, but carried the same hue of oppression this day.

Bottom of the second

Dock stepped back onto the mound. The light had cooled to a sickly yellow. The sky over San Diego bled into purple haze.

The Umpire was waiting again, crouched like a marionette at rest. Dock tried to ignore him, to focus on the ball, but the pulse had grown louder now, every seam a nerve ending.

He came set, drew a breath.

The Umpire straightened, pointing before Dock even moved. "Strike one."

Dock froze. "I haven't thrown yet."

The Umpire's head tilted, a small giggle escaping from behind the mask.

"Strike two," he said.

Dock looked toward May, who motioned for calm. "Dock, he called it a strike. Settle in. Let's go."

"He can't call what I haven't thrown."

"Then throw it," May said, mask already down.

Dock did. The ball left his hand with a hiss.

The Umpire's arm went up before it reached the plate. "Strike three."

The crowd applauded politely, unaware.

Dock's throat tightened. He turned toward the plate. "You don't get to call the future."

The Umpire laughed, soft, bright, perfectly sane. "Future's over, Ellis. It's already been scored."

Dock stepped off, shaking his head. He looked to the scoreboard for something fixed, something human.

It was blank.

No runs, no hits, no errors. No inning markers. No clock.

Just the shadow of the scoreboard attendant standing in the high window, motionless, watching him.

Dock felt the ball twitch once in his palm.

Then the lights along the outfield wall flickered and went out.

CHAPTER SEVEN

The Inning That Forgot Him

The inning began with a small mercy. Dock found a groove that felt like something earned rather than granted. He set his heel, let his hips lead, and the arm followed. The ball left clean. Strike one, chest high. A noise rose from the dugout that sounded like confidence.

He repeated the motion. Strike two at the knees. The batter swayed and stared and then walked away shaking his head. The next man swung through a fast one up and out. Two strikeouts on eight pitches. The crowd murmured in a new register, not mocking now, not even impatient, just attentive. Dock exhaled and rolled the ball into his glove. For a few breaths the world behaved like a field again.

Jerry met him halfway to the line. He tugged at the tape on his fingers the way a man might pull at a bad thought. The gauze had darkened where sweat soaked through. In the hard sun it looked pale from the salt, a chalky line across each knuckle.

"You seeing it?" Jerry asked, low enough for only Dock.

"Seeing it fine," Dock said. "It is seeing me."

Jerry nodded as if that were ordinary. "Keep your front side closed. You fly, you miss."

Dock looked at the tape again. The edges had frayed, thin threads catching light. For a second he thought the light came from the tape itself. Then a shadow crossed the rail and the gleam died. Ordinary after all.

They reached the grass and split. Jerry peeled left toward the plate. Dock slipped into the dugout where the air tasted of dust and tobacco and wintergreen. He set himself on the bench, elbows to knees, head down. The heartbeat in his palm had quieted. He closed his hand hard just to test it. Nothing. Only skin on leather. The quiet felt like a truce.

Across from him, Bill Mazeroski flexed both knees and winced. He rubbed his right one with the heel of his hand, working the ache as if it could be reasoned with. Years had stacked on that joint like innings that never ended. He never complained. He simply measured what was left and dealt the hand.

Stargell told a story with his hands. Sunflower shells clicked against wood as he talked, a soft rain on planks. His voice filled the dugout without rising. A teammate from the minors, a bus that had never truly stopped, a game that ended with three swings and a bad hop. Laughter rolled and then settled. Willie always found the heat in a room and gave it to others.

Clemente stood apart, not aloof, simply composed. He watched Dock without staring, the way a captain watches the horizon, trusting the men but not the weather. The set of his jaw said patience. The eyes said work.

The dugout felt lighter for once. Two strikeouts, a clean inning, and the rhythm of the game back under his feet. For the first time all night, the bench exhaled as one.

The old bullpen phone rattled once, then stopped. Bartirome reached for it out of habit, listened, and frowned. "Wrong line," he said, setting it down again. "Press box chatter bleeding through."

Dock looked up from his glove. "What'd they say?"

Tony shrugged. "Couldn't tell. Just a hum. Maybe the scoreboard calling for a fix."

Murtaugh didn't glance over. "Then fix it," he muttered.

The bench laughed once, too quickly, the way men laugh when something small reminds them they're still here. Dock smiled thinly and went back to rubbing the ball, tracing the seams like a map he had to memorize all over again.

Tony nodded and moved on to a rookie with a tight forearm and eyes too wide for a man who had been paid to play since spring.

Murtaugh's voice came from the far end. "Stay tall, Ellis. Do not reach."

Murtaugh never begged and he never asked. He directed. It was a language Dock understood even when he did not like it. The manager had a bullpen to ration and a second game to finish tonight. There were always two clocks running in Murtaugh's head. One for the inning. One for the week. He tapped the lineup card with his forefinger and glanced toward right, as if Clemente's presence could be counted like a pitch.

Jerry slid onto the bench beside Dock and wrapped new tape around his fingers. He did it without looking down, eyes on the field as he wound and tore and pressed. The tape came off the roll pale, then turned gray where sweat kissed it.

"Tell me something, Dock," Jerry said. "You seeing the ball better now, or is it lying to you and telling you it is better."

"It is clean," Dock said. "Cleaner than it's been all day."

Jerry grunted. "I am losing it for a split second halfway. It blinks, then comes back to me. Might be glare. Might be my eyes. Might be you."

"Might be the air, Jerry." Dock said. "Feels thick. Like something moved in."

Jerry wiped his palm on his thigh. "Air is air. We play in it."

"This air's got a mood."

Jerry looked at him then, but not with fear and not with pity. It was with something not every catcher has. That's a catcher's accounting. This man can do the thing or he cannot. This man is telling the truth or he is telling himself a story that will keep him whole. Jerry knew what to look for. If he didn't see it, he knew what to ask. And just when his pitcher thought he had all the answer, Jerry changed the questions.

"You keep the ball where I show," Jerry said. "Whatever mood the air has, it will take care of itself."

Dock nodded. He did not trust the promise, but he trusted the mouth that made it. All the confidence Dock had in Manny, he now had tenfold in Jerry May.

They took the field again. The sun had slid behind the upper deck. The light that reached the grass came in at a low angle and turned the outfield to glass. Dock stood on the mound and stared into that pane. He felt small. The feeling was not comfort. The task at hand, however, felt necessary.

He threw a first-pitch curve that never quite bit. Ball one. He chased with a fastball up and in that ate at the hands. Foul back. The next pitch sank late. A soft roller toward third died on the grass and rolled into Robertson's glove like a tame animal. Out by 3 steps. The rhythm settled into something that felt like routine work rather than danger.

Between pitches he glanced at Jerry's hands. Fresh tape. New color. No glow. But when Jerry set the target, the gauze made a small square of white inside the leather, a lighthouse in a bay of brown. It drew the eye even when Dock tried to keep his focus on the pocket. He used it the way men use stars. Not for the light itself. For what the light implied.

He fanned the next hitter on three. The last swing cut air. Dock heard the sound of a man missing something by inches and knowing it. He liked that sound. It said he was not the only one adjusting to a world that had shifted a degree.

The third out came on another strikeout, a fastball away that looked like a gift and then ran off the table. Jerry stood and threw the ball toward the dugout with a small snap of the wrist that said, yes, this is craft, not magic.

In the tunnel, Clemente stopped Dock with a hand to the chest. Not rough. Not soft. Simply firm enough to halt a man moving too fast.

"You play like a man fighting God," Clemente said.

Dock's answer came before his mind weighed it. "Maybe I am."

Clemente considered this for the length of a breath. The muscles at the corner of his jaw changed. Not a smile. Not a frown. The faint acknowledgment that a truth had been spoken out loud.

"Then pitch like you mean to win," he said. "Do not perform your doubt. Throw it."

Dock nodded. "Okay, Bobby."

Clemente's eyes held his another second, then slid past him toward the field. Duty reclaimed him. He walked on.

Back on the bench the story shifted. Stargell had gone quiet. He watched Dock over the top of his glove. The warmth in him never left, but calculation joined it. He knew what it meant for a team when a pitcher both lost and found himself in the same night. He had seen victories that won a series and broke a man. He had seen losses that hardened a spine. He tried to measure which path tonight had chosen.

Mazeroski rolled his shoulders once, then stood and stretched until his spine popped. He checked the dirt on his cleats as if dirt could tell the future.

Murtaugh stood with one hand on the bat rack, eyes on the field and on the bullpen and on Dock all at once. A manager lives at three distances. He never lets himself stand fully in any of them.

The phone buzzed once, sharp and insistent. Bartirome lifted the receiver, listened, then turned. "For you."

Dock frowned. "Who's calling?"

Tony shrugged. "Didn't say."

He handed it over. The line breathed like it had been waiting for him.

A voice came through — low, steady, with the weight of someone used to being heard. "You throw like you're asking the world to explain itself."

Dock blinked. "Who is this?"

"You already know."

The tone was familiar, but the name wouldn't rise. A warmth behind the words, an authority that pressed against his chest like a heartbeat remembered.

"You think they'll ever see you right?" the voice asked.

Dock's throat tightened. "That ever happen for anybody?"

A pause. Then, quietly: "Then make them look."

The line clicked off.

He held the receiver another moment, waiting for something more, but all that came back was the hiss of the crowd above them, distant and indifferent. Dock set the phone down slow, careful not to let it clatter.

Tony glanced over. "Skip checking on you again?"

Dock's voice came flat. "Guess we'll see."

The next half-inning began with a walk that tested patience. Four close pitches that felt like arguments the plate would not entertain. Jerry stopped at the edge of the mound and tapped the back of Dock's glove with the ball.

"You're fine," he said. "Hold your lane."

Before Dock could answer, the Umpire's voice cracked across the diamond.

"Anytime you boys want to *play baseball*, I'll be right here!"

His tone wasn't loud enough for the crowd, just sharp enough for them. The mask tilted, sunlight flashing off the bars.

Jerry glanced toward the plate, jaw tight. "We're coming."

The Umpire spread his arms in mock patience. "Take your time, gentlemen. Game's all yours. For now."

Dock felt the words hang heavier than they should have. For now. The way he said it wasn't about pace. It was about outcome.

Jerry turned back, voice low. "Ignore him."

"Hard to, when he's calling the game," Dock said.

"Then make him call it your way."

Jerry started back toward the plate. The mask dipped once, then disappeared behind the crouch.

Dock stared after him, the sound of the Umpire's last word still alive in his head.

A fly to shallow left found Stargell without fuss. The next batter chopped one toward second. Mazeroski charged, gloved it clean, and turned in one motion. The throw to first skipped once in the dirt but Oliver scooped it smooth, his toe hugging the bag.

Out. Two down.

The ump hesitated just long enough to make Dock's pulse jump before signaling with a lazy fist.

A small leak of frustration developed behind Dock's teeth. Not at the call — at how close everything felt, like the game itself was testing the edges of perfection just to see if he'd flinch.

He swallowed it.

The batter who came next carried himself like a man who had not been told what kind of game he was in. He took a long look at Dock and then at the Umpire and then back at Dock. He dug his cleat and left a clean trench. The mark looked like an arrow pointing toward the mound.

Jerry put down one finger and did not move. Fastball, simple, challenge, trust me.

Dock nodded and came set. The seam bit into the pad of his thumb in a way that felt personal. He lifted, stepped, turned, and released. The pitch ran inside. Not by much. Enough to take the batter on the frontside elbow.

The sound was a hollow thud that lived more in bone than in air. The crowd made the sound a crowd makes when another man's body is struck. A long oh that blends concern and appetite.

The batter folded, then straightened with a curse that sounded like a prayer. He walked to first with his chest out. Pride makes a man taller when he hurts.

Dock watched him and felt something slide sideways inside his head. The man's face blurred into his own for a blink, not a vision over the world, not a mask laid across another, just a quick reflection in a piece of glass that might have been air or might have been nothing. The man tipped his cap to acknowledge that a clip to the funny bone is anything but funny but Dock couln't blink his face off the runner's body.

He turned away, then turned back fast. The runner at first looked ordinary again. The moment had passed. The bruise would flower under the short sleeves. The game would proceed.

May walked the ball to the mound. He stood close enough that Dock could smell leather and salt.

"You are fine," Jerry said. "Do not go looking for meaning."

"I hit another one, God damn it," Dock said. "Are they ever pulling me?"

"You threw inside," Jerry said. "He stood in. We are even. And no, they're not pulling you as long as there's a second game."

Dock breathed, in and out. The air went down like a drink he did not order, then settled.

From shallow right field, Clemente called something in Spanish too fast for English ears. Dock heard the shape of it, not the words. It sounded like caution married with respect.

Murtaugh raised a hand and lowered it, a signal as old as a dugout. Keep your mind where your feet are. Finish the frame.

Dock took the sign and sank a curve at the knees. Strike one, and the Umpire's call arrived like a note written by a precise hand. Another curve, wider. Ball one. He climbed the ladder and got the swing he wanted. Foul back into the seats. A fastball away ended it. The bat died in air. Three outs.

He walked off slow. The sound around him was thin now, as if the park had forgotten a line it meant to sing.

He looked to the dugout and saw Murtaugh take his spot near the steps. Next to him sat another Dock, or the suggestion of one superimposed and almost sitting on Murtaugh's shoulder. Was he the angel or the devil? The grin in the air like a grease mark on clean glass said this was no benign apparition. Dock blinked hard and the bench looked normal again. A batboy chewed at a thumbnail. Stargell talked low to Robertson at third. Clemente tugged at the bill of his cap, once, precise.

For a heartbeat Dock heard a whisper behind his ear that did not disturb the air.

"He is done, Skip. Pull him."

Murtaugh did not turn his head. He stared at the field. The hand that had been on the bat rack flexed once. Managers hear a thousand voices in a night. Most belong to the living.

Dock stopped at the top step. A part of him, old and tired, wanted that hand to reach for the hook. Rest sounded like a shore he had not seen in months. Silence promised a kind of health the body could taste and never quite keep.

Another part knew that if he left now, the game would continue without him and take his name with it. He would live, but something he had carried since boyhood would not.

He closed his hand around the ball. The seams pulsed once against his palm. Not a miracle. A reminder.

Jerry brushed past him and slapped his shoulder with the back of his glove. "You are not done."

"Say it again," Dock said.

"You are not done," Jerry said. "If you are tired, lean on me. I will see the next two for you."

Dock nodded and stepped down. The dugout floor was wood and concrete and gum and sun. It held him the way a good sentence holds the truth for a while.

Clemente caught his eye as he passed. There was nothing soft in that look. Only agreement. Pitch like you mean to win. Then he was gone, a white number moving toward the outfield where the edges of the day had started to bruise.

Stargell flicked a seed that bounced off Dock's shoe. "Bring us back in quick," he said. "I got something cooking."

Murtaugh did not look at Dock. He did not need to. He spoke to the air in front of him and to a man he had kept on a card for a reason.

"Get your breath," he said. "You are back out."

Dock took it like a command and like a gift. He sat. He breathed. The phone stayed quiet. The crowd made a sound like water working under a pier. The Umpire adjusted his mask at home and for an instant seemed to look into the dugout through steel bars that caught the last light and made small suns.

Dock squeezed the ball once more and stood.

The inning waited. The night pressed closer. The line between control and surrender narrowed to the width of a seam.

He stepped up the tunnel and felt the field receive him.

The mirror on the bench, if there had been one, left no trace.

Only the game remained, and the work.

And the voice that belonged to him alone, steady now in his chest, saying what he needed to hear.

Finish.

Dock came set, more out of muscle memory than focus. The motion was clean, unthinking. The ball left his hand and vanished into the dark between mound and plate. For an instant it hung there, spinning without sound, without place, every stitch holding its own light.

He blinked. The air changed temperature. The crowd noise folded into crickets and water. Dock was no longer in his element. He was no longer on the field.

Chapter Eight

You Always End Where You Begin

Dock blinked and the smell told him first. Mud and hot iron. River breath and rot. Frogs throbbed in the dark. Dock stood beside a parked truck with its engine ticking down. The door was open. A flashlight burned a white hole in the night and carved two men into hard shapes.

"Get him," said one.

They dragged a boy from the truck bed, small and kicking, the loose heel of a shoe slapping metal. Dock moved before he thought. His hands went out to take weight, to say wait, to say this is a child. A palm shoved his chest. He reeled and caught himself on the fender. The steel was hot like a fever.

The boy looked at Dock. The whites of his eyes shone too bright in the beam. He tried for a smile and missed it. "They said I whistled," he whispered. The words were smoke.

The night carried no help. Trees held their breath. The men did not look at Dock again. They hauled the boy down the path toward water. Brush scraped legs. Someone's heel skidded and a curse snapped the air in two.

Dock ran as his lungs burned. The beam of the light cut the reeds and found the muddy river. It showed the face of the smaller man, white and strained, then lost it again in black. The boy begged. Hands and cloth subdued him as he begged, pleaded for freedom. Dock reached for a shoulder and grabbed nothing. His fingers closed on air cold enough to bite. He tried again and found only wet leaves and the slick twist of vine.

He screamed. It came out wrong. The sound barely made it past his tongue but died at his teeth.

A splash. Then a second, heavier. The current took what it was given. Dock hit the bank on his knees and clawed at the water. The river pushed his hands away like an animal that did not want to be touched.

Behind him a voice said, "Time."

Not loud. Not caring. A clerk closing a ledger.

Dock turned. A man in dark clothes stood at the path, a black mask in his hand that was not a mask for this world. He did not put it on. He did not need to. His face was ordinary and dry and patient. He raised one finger as if pausing a conversation and lowered it again.

"I always call it clean," he said.

Dock went for him and found only reeds. The path emptied. The light snapped shut. The frogs kept singing. The boy, gone.

He closed his eyes until he saw shapes. Suddenly, his shoes were on tile. The air was stale and hot with breath and wool. A hundred people pressed in rows of metal chairs. Dock stood at the back of a hall where a man in a tie spoke from a low stage. The man's voice was quick and exact. It found the corners of the room and lit them. Dock did not know the words yet, only the shape of them. He leaned to hear better and missed the first movement near the exit doors.

A shout. Then a figure surged up the aisle with a hand inside a coat. Dock pushed through arms and backs and a woman's purse that snapped open and spilled a comb and a small bottle. He grabbed for the man's sleeve. The cloth slid like oil under his fingers.

Fire broke the room.

The speaker folded and the stage seemed to dip around him. People flattened to the floor. A woman screamed and did not stop. Another man shouted for a doctor and there was no doctor. Dock climbed onto the lip of the stage and slid on blood that traveled faster than any bullet. He knelt and pressed both hands to a wound that breathed against his palms.

"I can help you," Dock said. It sounded childish in his own ears.

The man on the floor tried to speak. His mouth shaped the start of a word that might have been light. His eyes flicked once to Dock's face and seemed to know it. Dock pressed harder. Another shot cracked across the hall. Someone stepped on Dock's back and knocked him forward. His cheek hit the slick floor. When he lifted his head his hands shone the color of varnish.

Cameras flashed. Dock looked up. For half a second the black grid of a mask hovered in the white glare, just a trick of lines where metal chairs met shadows. The mask smiled without a mouth.

"Strike," said a voice behind the flash. The word was not for a game. It was a note taken in a small book.

Dock swung his arm at air. Fingers closed on empty light. The flashes kept coming. People ran. The sound became a single never-ending breath. The man on the floor looked smaller now, and far away, and already on a stamp.

He pushed through the stampede, lungs raw from smoke and fear, slipping in blood he couldn't tell was his own. Someone grabbed at his jacket; he tore free and shoved through the side door into the street.

The cold air hit him like a fist. Sirens pulsed far away, uneven and wrong, and the sky above Harlem bent in strange colors that no city light could make. He ran without knowing where—down an alley that seemed to tilt and breathe, past trash fires that smelled like burning plastic and sugar.

He looked back once. The door he'd come through was gone. In its place was another street, flat and wide, lined with palm trees and smoke. The skyline had changed. The air was hotter. He wasn't in New York anymore.

He coughed bile and glass. Sirens yelped. The night was orange but the sky above was still dark, as if the fire had not convinced heaven. He stood in the middle of a street that ran wide and straight between low stores with iron gates halfway down. A bottle arced from a rooftop and broke on a police cruiser parked crooked at the curb. The flame breathed at once and found something to eat.

A boy ran past Dock with tape wrapped around his knuckles and rage in his teeth. Dock grabbed his forearm. The skin was hot and slick.

"Don't," Dock said. "You are giving them the story they want."

The boy looked at him and Dock saw his own eyes. Younger, unscarred, the whites too bright in the burning air. "You already wrote it," the boy said, and tore free.

Glass rained like bright hail. A woman cried in a window. Dock flinched as a display of dresses took fire and shrank into black shapes that still tried to be women. A helmeted officer swung a baton into a man's ribs and then again, as if making sure. The man fell without sound and Dock's stomach flipped like a coin.

At the corner a figure used two orange cones to wave traffic, left hand up, right hand down, the motion slow and graceful in the smoke. He wore no uniform. He wore a black shell over his chest that caught the firelight and gave none back.

"Keep moving," he sang, light and bright, turning his wrists. "Use the crosswalk, children."

Dock walked toward him. Heat climbed his legs through his trousers. "Stop it," Dock said. "They are going to kill somebody."

The man's mask turned. It reflected the whole world and none of it. "Fair is whatever stays within the lines," he said. "Try not to trip."

Dock lunged but fell to his face. The man stepped away and the corner emptied, cones and all, as if the smoke had eaten him.

When Dock regained his feet and felt them on the painted concrete, he noticed paint in the shape of a number you could see from the sky. He looked up at the motel balcony and saw a man laugh at a joke someone had told. The laugh was full and soft. The air had gooseflesh. A second man in a tie pointed at heaven, not a sermon, just a gesture about weather maybe.

Dock climbed the steps two at a time. He knew what came next because the skin on his arms turned cold all at once and he wanted to throw up. He put out his hand and said wait to a stranger who was not listening. Somewhere across a parking lot a muzzle winked once. A sound cracked. The man in the tie jerked forward and fell like someone had pulled string from his spine.

Dock got there before the body settled. He caught the weight against his chest and slid down the wall with it. He had never held a man who was leaving. It felt like catching water with your hands. It felt like trying to keep a door from closing when the whole house wants it shut.

"I can help," Dock said. "Stay. Please."

The man's mouth worked. His hand found Dock's sleeve and held it even after it could not hold. The eyes were open and not seeing. Dock pressed his forehead to the man's shoulder and said a prayer he did not know he remembered.

Footsteps banged up the stairs. Voices scattered like coins. Dock looked up and saw a man in a black chest protector standing in the motel doorway as if it were a tunnel to someplace cooler. The chest piece gleamed in the ugly light. In his hand he held a small clicker. He pressed the steel tongue and Dock heard the tiny count.

One. Two. Three.

"You could have stopped it," Dock said. His voice was raw. "You were here."

"If I stop it, who tallies the world," the man said. He sounded pleased without smiling. "Someone must keep it playable."

"Playable," Dock said, and the word made something inside him tear.

The man stepped forward and for the first time Dock saw his face clearly. He was nobody. He could have been a clerk at a window that sold you stamps. His eyes were the color of dishwater. He smelled like sun and talk radio and coffee that had stopped being hot an hour ago. He lifted the mask as if to scratch his cheek and then settled it back down again, careful not to smudge anything.

"You always end where you begin," he said. "That is the mercy. No one gets lost. No one gets out."

Dock let the dead man's arm slide from his grip. He stood. His hands shook and left brown prints on his trousers.

"Then I will break the beginning," he said. "I will throw until the stitch comes loose."

"That is what keeps it going," the man said, and the hall light above his head clicked once, off and on, as if applauding.

Sound dropped out of the world. Then it returned as a single long tone that Dock knew too well. He squeezed his eyes shut and dirt pressed under his spikes. The crowd was back. The smell of hot peanuts and cut grass came home. Night had fallen and the lights made the outfield look like water you could walk on if you did not think about it too hard.

Home plate waited. The man in the black mask crouched there, small now, proportionate to a game. He looked up only once, not to Dock, not to anyone, just to the idea of a rule.

Jerry set himself and put down a sign. It was as plain as a doorknob. Dock nodded. His body knew what to do. His head did not trust any of it. The morning's acid hadn't ruined him; it had stripped him clean. The LSD peeled away the noise that let men pretend the world made sense. He could see the truth now, the scaffolding behind everything and how each motion, each breath, each rule was held together by threads so thin they cried when touched. It was both enlightenment and exposure. The drug had done what truth always does when it shows its teeth: it left him seeing too much to ever shut his eyes again.

He came set. The ball was warm. He felt the raised seams against his index finger and thumb like a vein under skin. The first motion began in his heel and traveled clean through bone and muscle into the shoulder. He could hear his breath and the little animal sound the leather made when it turned over on itself.

"Remember," said a voice, not loud, not kind. "You always end where you begin."

Dock did not answer. He took the breath he had trained since childhood to take. He let the hand come through the window his coaches had made for him when he was a boy and too green to know what he carried. He saw a path narrow to the width of a song. He let go.

The ball cut the air like a key.

A man in the third row laughed at something his date said. A girl near the foul pole wrote her name in the condensation on a cup. A cop on the aisle ate a hot dog and blotted his fingers on his napkin and then his trouser leg. Somewhere in the upper deck a transistor radio caught half a sentence and then lost it to static.

Dock watched the ball slide into a world that had tried to end him before he started. He watched it find the place that was made for it and no other. He did not look at the man in the black mask. He did not look at the clock. He looked only where the leather had to go.

The sound of a struck truth rang in his chest.

He did not feel triumph. He felt balance. A string pulled tight across a canyon that had swallowed better men and would swallow him too. Not tonight. Not now. He set his foot, asked for the next sign, and heard the crowd become a single animal again, breathing with him.

"Again," he told himself, and the word was a prayer.

From behind the plate the Arbiter said nothing. He did not giggle. He did not sing. He watched and counted and waited for the moment when all beginnings meet their ends and start again.

Dock kept throwing. The night stayed stitched. For the span of a few pitches, the world held.

CHAPTER NINE

The Weight of His Name

From the on-deck circle, the air still smelled of tobacco, sweat, and slow-burning hope. Clemente stood alone at dead center, head bowed, hands folded around his bat like it was an instrument meant for prayer. In the dugout, Dock carved silence into the cement. Every few seconds the crowd's noise rose, broke, and fell again. It reminded Clemente of waves that never reached the shore.

He had been quiet most of the game, speaking only when necessary. Words did not travel well in dugouts. They hit the walls and bounced back changed, like echoes that forgot what they were answering to.

"Two away here in the top of the fourth, Dave Roberts working smooth tonight... and that brings the great Roberto Clemente to the plate. Three thousand hits in his future, no doubt about that." declared the radio announcer. "Now batting, right fielder, number twenty-one... Roberto Clemente." confirmed the public address.

Dave Roberts stood on the mound, small and taut as wire. A good pitcher, patient, more machine than man. The kind who threw the same pitch four times until you made a mistake. Clemente watched him and saw the game shrinking, rules tightening around rhythm, calculation replacing courage. Baseball had become an accountant's art, every move measured against the ledger of probability. Roberts thrived in that world. Clemente never had.

The inning turned, and his name was called.

He rose slowly, as if motion itself had become sacred. He adjusted his gloves, tapped the bat once against his spikes, and stepped toward the light. The dugout faded behind him, the smell of liniment and dust giving way to the clean sting of sunlight on grass.

The first pitch came high and hard, brushing him back. The crowd gasped. He did not flinch. Roberts was not throwing at him. He was testing posture, asking whether the old man still had the balance to stand his ground.

Between them stretched ninety feet of geometry and deceit. Pitcher and hitter, two craftsmen working the same illusion from opposite sides. The ball was not just speed; it was conversation, each release a sentence thrown into doubt. The hitter tried to read intent in the smallest tremor of a wrist, the pitcher tried to write destiny in seams and spin. Every game was an argument about who owned time, the man who began motion or the man who ended it.

Clemente had spent his life answering that argument. To him, hitting was faith disguised as timing. You waited for the pitch that believed in you as much as you believed in it. Roberts had his own religion, one built on control and the refusal to leave anything to faith.

But there was a third presence in that narrow corridor of air, something older than the rules that defined it. The space between mound and plate carried its own watcher, invisible and patient, a will that neither pitcher nor hitter could sense but both obeyed. It waited in the pulse of the seams, in the brief hush before contact, in the unspoken promise that every ball thrown had already chosen where it would end.

Roberts thought he was dictating the game. Clemente thought he was defying it. Neither understood they were performing a script written long before the first pitch left his hand.

The catcher muttered something in English that Clemente half-heard, half-imagined. An insult about age, or about accent. The words slid past, but they left a film. Ironic in a city with a Spanish name.

He knew Roberts. Men like that never meant to challenge you just once. When they brushed you back high and tight, it was not a pitch. It was a question. *Will you flinch the next time I try?* Roberts wanted to trap him in that moment of doubt, to carve a small wound in confidence and let it bleed slow. That was the secret art of control: not command of the ball, but command of the man holding the bat.

Clemente had faced that kind of challenge his whole life. It came dressed as fastballs, headlines, customs officers, and contract negotiations. Each one carried the same voice underneath: *Step back. Know your place.* But he had learned that the strike zone was not just a box painted in chalk. It was the measure of a man's refusal.

He gripped the bat tighter, fingers remembering the weight of poverty, the sting of winter leagues, the sound of English spoken like a weapon. The next time another fastball came for his chest, he would not protect. He would punish.

Somewhere above the diamond, beyond the lights, the air shifted. The invisible third thing that ruled the space between pitcher and hitter leaned closer, curious. It liked the rhythm of defiance, the old push and pull of fear and pride. Every act of courage bent the threads of its unseen order, and Clemente's resolve drew the smallest ripple across the field.

Neither man noticed the change. Roberts saw only the target, the chest he meant to test again. Clemente saw only the next chance to answer. Between them, the unseen force coiled tighter, feeding on the friction, waiting for the moment when faith and control would meet and one of them would crack.

The second pitch sank low, tight against the knee. Strike one. Clemente stepped away, rolled his shoulders, and nodded once. The umpire's voice was clean, impartial, yet carried something smug beneath it. He had heard that tone before—from reporters, from bureaucrats, from men who pronounced his name wrong even after he corrected them. Every call in this country had a little lesson inside it.

The third pitch curved in late, barely missing his ribs. The crowd booed, wanting outrage. He refused to give it. Dignity was not for show. He dusted the dirt from his pants and thought of his father cutting cane beneath the Caribbean sun, never looking up even when the overseer barked. Work was its own argument. The man who bends without breaking wins more than the man who screams.

Roberts came again. The fourth pitch nicked the outside corner. Strike two. The sound of the ball in the catcher's glove was crisp and final. The crowd exhaled as one body.

Clemente turned to the umpire. "He missed by a hand."

The catcher grinned through his mask. "Not today, old man."

Clemente said nothing, but something in his chest went taut. He stepped back in, weight balanced, eyes fixed.

The fifth pitch came quick, a fastball. He met it and fouled it off, straight back, the sound sharp as a slap against concrete. The sixth pitch was another curve, dipping low, asking him to chase it. He watched it drop out of the zone and let it pass. Ball three.

He stepped back, wiped his palms on his pants, and exhaled. The sunlight had shifted. The shadows of the upper deck crept toward the plate, long fingers reaching for his cleats. Roberts kicked the dirt from his spikes and waited for the sign. The crowd was restless now, a living tide murmuring his name in a dozen broken versions. Clem-en-tee. Cle-men-tay. Each one a reminder of how far language could wander from its home and still be asked to serve.

The duel stretched while time lost its edges. Each throw was a sentence in a language both men spoke but never the same way. Roberts pitched in numbers and angles. Clemente replied in patience.

The seventh pitch cut close to his hands. He turned just enough to foul it off, the sound a short, hard echo that died in the air. The next came faster, a little higher. Another foul, looping into the crowd. The count stayed full, the battle feeding on itself.

Roberts worked slower now, holding the ball between fingers slick with sweat. He stared at the plate as if trying to memorize Clemente's heartbeat.

The ninth pitch came low, a sharp breaking ball. Clemente went down with it, knees bent, and clipped it off the end of the bat. The ball spun backward, striking the dirt at his feet and bouncing away. The crowd murmured, restless and reverent.

The tenth pitch came high and tight, the challenge he had expected since the first. He turned on it, quick and violent, and for an instant the crack sounded like deliverance. The ball rose, perfect, climbing toward right field, white against the sky. Clemente watched it arc into the sun, a line too clean to be doubted.

For that climb, everything he knew about the game felt true again. The balance of patience and rage. The muscle memory that had carried him from Carolina to Pittsburgh.

The thousand mornings of soft hands and hard swings. This one felt like the reward waiting at the end of all those small obediences.

His eyes tracked the ball climbing higher. The crowd noise fell away. Behind him, someone shouted, "There it goes!" Another voice cut through, "Ah, shit. God damn it, Roberts!" as the Padres' faith broke like glass.

The white blur reached its highest point and began to fall, curving just enough to betray him. He watched the fade, slow and beautiful, the kind of failure that almost looked divine.

Then the umpire's arm turned, slow and theatrical, pointing foul.

The world snapped back into noise. The roar collapsed into protest. Padres fans cheered. Pirates fans cursed. Clemente's heartbeat slowed. His hands tightened on the bat until his knuckles paled.

The catcher leaned close. "You almost got it out of here, viejo."

Clemente did not look at him. "Every story ends the same."

The catcher blinked. "And how's that?"

"Foul."

He picked up the bat, brushed dirt from the barrel, and stepped back in. He no longer waited for the next high fastball. He invited it.

The eleventh pitch came in flat. Clemente met it square and sent it straight back, a missile that clanged off the backstop and dropped dead. Another foul.

The twelfth came quick, almost cruel, a fastball running high and away. He chased it, connection just off-center. The ball flared to shallow left, a dying arc. The shortstop backpedaled, glove raised.

Caught.

Out.

The park exhaled as one. Polite applause broke through the silence. It was the kind of out that still looked heroic in the dugout.

As Clemente lowered the bat, someone in the stands shouted, "Sit down, twenty-one!" Another voice followed, softer, "You're still the best, Roberto." The mix of praise and contempt twisted together until it was impossible to tell which stung more.

He started his walk back to the dugout. The umpire's mask followed him, still and expressionless. As he passed, the man's voice slipped low enough for only Clemente to hear.

"Even the clean ones bend foul in the end."

Clemente stopped. "Not forever."

"Forever doesn't end when you say so," the umpire said.

He paused at the edge of the dirt, turned back toward the plate, and spoke softly, words meant for the one voice that claimed authority here.

"One day," he said, "you'll have to call me safe right here at home plate."

The umpire remained silent. The crowd roared for the next batter, already forgetting.

Clemente descended the steps, set his bat down gently, and sat. He watched Dock stretch his arm, jaw tight, preparing to return to the mound. Clemente looked at him and thought about how the game and the world both asked men like them to be flawless just to be seen.

He untied the tape on his wrist, rewound it tighter, and whispered, "Haz tu deber siempre." Always do your duty.

Then he looked back at the field, where order still pretended to hold, and waited for the sound of Dock's next pitch cutting the lie in half.

CHAPTER TEN

Pops and the Shape of Light

The crowd settled into a low, rolling hum, the sound of thousands of lungs exhaling together. Dock Ellis walked back to the mound. The air over San Diego Stadium pulsed with light too clean to be real. For a few seconds, he thought he could see the beams moving, searching, the way prison lights do when something's escaped. He rolled the ball in his hand, and the seams crawled faintly under his fingers like veins alive and aware.

The Umpire spoke again, though no air moved in the space between them. "You fight hard," the voice said, a slow vibration that bypassed the ear. "You think effort rewrites truth. It doesn't. The players change. The rules do not."

Dock looked toward home plate. The Umpire stood motionless, mask glinting black, chest protector rising and falling with no visible breath. Behind him, the crowd swayed in its own rhythm, half shadow, half light.

He toed the rubber. The noise fell away until he could hear only his heartbeat. He threw the first pitch. The ball cut the air and split into sound instead of motion like a distorted chord from a feedback loop.

The batter blinked. For a flicker, his Padres uniform shifted to a purple coat, white scarf, a flash of electric hair. The bat became a guitar neck, the pickguard gleaming like polished bone. "*Jimi?*", Dock thought. The face smiled, teeth too bright, eyes wide and knowing. Then it was gone, just a man in gold and white. Dock threw again, the sound bending with it.

Each pitch came like music. The first, distortion. The second, bass. The third, a long screaming note that hovered in midair before crashing into the catcher's mitt. "Strike three!"

Dock exhaled, but it didn't feel like a win. The sound in his head still hummed, a frequency too low for the world to hear.

"You keep trying to change the song," the Umpire said. "It only ever plays one tune." he continued.

Dock ignored him and reached for the rosin bag. His breath came sharp, the white dust falling through his fingers like static. He wound and fired again. The next hitter rolled a weak grounder to short, and for a moment Dock's vision blurred. The infield warped like heat off asphalt. The ball split in two, then four, each rolling in different directions. His body moved on instinct, one part watching, one part throwing, and then everything went black.

In the dark, the Umpire's voice kept talking. "You saw behind the curtain. Now you know what keeps the lights on. Leave the game, Dock Ellis. You don't belong here."

When Dock came to, his arm was extended in follow-through, glove pointed at first. The infield umpire's call cut through the haze—"OUT!" The crowd applauded softly, the sound of people who had seen nothing strange.

Dock blinked at his own hand. His fingers were trembling. Jerry May jogged the ball back to him, steady as ever. "Nice play," he said, voice ordinary. Dock nodded, pretending to understand how he'd made it.

Three outs.

The inning was over.

He walked back to the dugout, heartbeat pounding against his skull. Clemente's words looped in his mind: *You play like a man fighting God.* Dock thought maybe that wasn't right. Maybe he was fighting the only thing smaller than God, the thing that crept into rules and shadows and called itself fair.

The trainer offered him a cup of water. Dock shook his head. "Get that shit away from me, man.," he muttered. The trainer shrugged and moved on. Dock no longer trusted even the hands that held him, the voices that advised him, nor the faces who laughed with him.

The Pirates were coming to bat.

Dock sat at the far end of the bench, the world moving like it was underwater. Stargell stepped up from the on-deck circle, bat resting on his shoulder like a scepter. The crowd changed pitch, dropping from noise to reverence. Even the Padres fans quieted. Everyone knew what that swing could do.

"Bring it home, Pops!" someone yelled.

Dock's eyes tracked him as he walked to the plate. Stargell's size wasn't just physical, it was gravitational. At six-foot-two, one hundred ninety pounds, the world seemed to move around him. Roberts, the Padre pitcher, took a breath that looked more like a prayer.

Willie Stargell was the anchor of the Pirates' ship and its rising myth. In 1970, he wasn't just the heart of the team;

he was the quiet engine that kept it human. While Dock burned and Clemente carried himself like a prophet, Stargell steadied everyone else with a laugh that could shake the dugout walls and a swing that could break cities. He had already started turning Forbes Field into a graveyard for pitchers. Out west, they said he hit balls that never came down, that there were baseballs orbiting the moon with his name stitched into them.

To the younger Pirates, he was both brother and sermon, discipline wrapped in easy warmth. He told rookies not to measure a season by averages but by the people you carried through it. He handed out hitting advice like parables. *You don't swing hard,* he'd say, *you swing true.* When the team bus went quiet after a loss, Stargell was the one who got them laughing again.

Around the league, there were men who swore they could still feel the wind from his bat days later, the air bent wrong by its arc. Dock had seen it himself. He saw how a game could change the moment Stargell's shadow stretched across home plate.

That was what he meant to Pittsburgh. Not just a slugger. A proof of life. A reminder that a man could stand in the dirt of this world and still swing like he believed in something better, bigger, or inexplicable.

Now he stood there again, the bat loose in his hands, body coiled, eyes bright and unafraid. The crowd shifted in tone, dropping from chatter to reverence. That reverence was due.

Roberts wound up, but the motion looked hesitant, almost deferential. He wasn't just facing a hitter. He was facing a force that reminded everyone how fragile order could be.

The first pitch came high and tight. Stargell didn't flinch. He let it pass, eyes never leaving the pitcher.

The second pitch, a curveball that could have dropped into a bucket meant to buckle his knees, but Stargell's swing unfolded like the beginning of a hymn.

Contact.

The sound wasn't a mere crack, but an explosion. The ball launched into the night, climbing higher than anything not manned by professional pilots. The stadium lights fluttered as if the current had broken. Dock stood, glove at his chest, watching it vanish into the black beyond left-center. The crowd rose to bear witness.

For an instant, everything went silent. The ball was gone. The sound, the crowd, even the hum inside Dock's head were all cut out. Then the lights flickered once, twice, and the ball reappeared beyond the fence.

Home run.

The roar came back too loud, stretched, unnatural. The scoreboard cards read **2–0, Pittsburgh.**

Dock felt the veins in his palm pulse with their own fever, each throb syncing with the flicker of the lights above. The seams of his undershirt felt like they were breathing against his skin. He looked toward home plate. The Umpire had not moved. But his shadow was still standing. The shape behind him was taller, broader, wrong. It quivered like something caught halfway between dimensions, its edges crawling. It moved even as the man did not.

The Umpire tilted his head slightly toward the dugout. His voice came cold, threaded through with something older than language. "You don't understand what you've done, Ellis. You opened a door you had no right to open."

Dock's stomach turned. The arteries in his neck tightened until they felt like piano wire ready to snap. His heartbeat climbed into his ears, a drumbeat he could not silence. Sweat ran cold down his ribs. He wanted to breathe, but every inhale felt borrowed and every exhale stolen.

He looked toward the field. Stargell was rounding second, smiling. The man looked untouchable, joy incarnate, a brief defiance of gravity and gods alike. The sound of his cleats striking dirt should have been solid, but it came to Dock like echoes underwater, muffled by a distance that was not real.

He wanted to yell, to warn him that the game had turned and that the rules had stopped belonging to them. But the words clotted in his throat. His tongue felt carved from the same leather as the ball.

The crowd roared again as Stargell crossed home plate. His teammates spilled from the dugout to greet him, laughing, slapping his shoulders. The sound hit Dock in waves that did not match the motion, laughter arriving seconds late, applause echoing before hands had moved.

Only Dock stayed still, staring at the Umpire crouching behind the plate, the mask glinting beneath lights that seemed to dim and brighten with his breathing.

The voice came again, low and satisfied, as if spoken from beneath the ground. "The rules hold the world together. You broke one."

Dock pressed his hand to his forehead. The skin there was cold, but beneath it something was moving, pulsing with the same tempo as the lights overhead. The world tilted, colors bleeding at the edges of vision. The white chalk lines stretched into rivers of light.

He looked up. The stars beyond the stadium lights were wrong. Too many. Too close. Too alive. They were watching, every point of light an open eye. His pulse matched the flicker of the bulbs, matched the heartbeat in his palm, matched the faint hum that rose through the grass and dirt beneath his spikes.

The field had become a breathing thing.

He whispered to himself, "The acid didn't make this."

It hadn't. It had only peeled back the cover that made the world tolerable. The real hallucination was the illusion of control, the game, the crowd, the chalk, the grass, the comfort of rules. Baseball was just the shape that power took here. In another life, it might have been a courtroom, a factory, a pulpit, a war. Whatever the stage, the universe found a way to make men dance, to let them believe they were calling the shots. But no one moved the needle.

For players like Dock, Willie, and Roberto, the field was only the latest lie. They ran, they hit, they pitched, they won, and they thought it mattered. It didn't. Not to whatever watched from beyond the lights.

And now he realized what Stargell's home run had done. It had not just cleared the wall. It had struck something behind it. Something that was never meant to be touched.

Dock's pulse slowed to a steady, deliberate rhythm. His breath felt too calm, too measured, as if his body knew it stood on the edge of a truth no man was built to hold.

"That swing might've ripped it open," he said, almost to himself.

The words disappeared into the dugout air, swallowed by the hum of lights that suddenly faltered. A flicker, a buzz, then darkness across the outfield.

For a heartbeat, the stadium was gone. No field, no players, no sound. Just the black, humming silence of a world without audience.

When the lights returned, the crowd came roaring back as if nothing had changed. But Dock looked up. The night sky was wrong.

A shape was moving across the moon. It was not a plane. It was too large, too deliberate, gliding as though gravity were a suggestion. The edges of it trailed into nothing, as if the thing were made of the space between light itself. The crowd never noticed.

Dock stood, his legs unsteady, the ball clenched so tightly his knuckles turned pale. The seams dug crescents into his palm. He could feel something in the ball pulsing back at him. Not life, but awareness.

The Umpire's voice slid through the static air. Calm. Patient. Amused.

"Now you'll know how insignificant you really are."

Dock smiled without humor. His teeth were clenched. His eyes stayed on the field, watching the world hold itself together for one more breath.

"Six more outs," he whispered. "And then we see who's keeping score."

The crowd cheered. The lights steadied. The shape above the moon vanished behind the clouds, but the air still vibrated with its presence.

Dock sat down again, the ball rolling between his fingers, alive with its own rhythm. He thought of the door, of the rules, of what it meant to finish a game that might never end.

The universe had started to notice him. And it was waiting.

CHAPTER ELEVEN

The Seams Open

The crowd's hum settled into one long note, stretched so thin it felt like it might tear. Dock stepped out of the dugout and felt the whole stadium inhale.

The grass did not look like grass anymore. Under the lights it had the sheen of wet skin. Each blade shivered as if something below it was breathing. The chalk lines pulsed faintly, not flashing like neon, just thickening and thinning, as if a vein ran under every stripe.

Six more outs.

He rolled the ball in his palm. The seams crawled against his skin, small ridges that felt less like stitching and more like a spine. His fingers fit between them as if they had always belonged there.

The Arbiter rose from his crouch behind the plate, slow and unhurried, like a man waking from a nap he did not need. The mask caught the light and swallowed it. The black of the chest protector seemed deeper now, the way a well looks deeper at midnight.

"You persist," the voice said.

The sound arrived inside Dock's skull. No breath. No throat. Just a vibration that turned thought into echo.

"You really want to finish this."

Dock spat into the dirt and rubbed the ball once more. "Came here to throw, old man."

"I am not old," the Arbiter said. "I am the part that never changes."

The Padres leadoff hitter for the seventh stepped into the box and scraped his cleats, unaware that the air itself had shifted. He adjusted his helmet and glanced at the stands, just another man in a uniform who wanted a hit.

Dock toed the rubber. His legs felt like they belonged to someone who had already pitched twelve innings. His arm felt like an arm that had never thrown at all, fresh and raw at the same time.

Jerry gave the sign. One finger, low and in. Dock nodded.

He came set. The mound rose under his back foot, then sank, then rose again as if it were treading water. He lifted, turned, and let the ball go.

The pitch left his hand and dragged a tail of light behind it. Not bright, just visible enough for his eye to catch. The seams turned, each stitch a thin red line that carved its own circle in the air.

"Ball one," the Arbiter said.

The pitch had started at the thigh, cut across the inside corner, and signed its name at the knees. Dock knew it. Jerry knew it. The batter stepped back and looked surprised that he had not swung.

Jerry popped from his crouch and walked the ball out to the mound.

"You missed a hair in," Jerry said.

"No, I did not," Dock said. His own voice sounded far away. "He did."

Jerry watched his eyes for a second. There was no comfort there, only calculation.

"Then hit the hair next time," Jerry said. "He is not giving you anything. So do not ask for anything."

He dropped the ball into Dock's glove and jogged back, tape bright on his fingers.

Dock rubbed the leather again. The hum in the air grew thicker. It pressed against his cheekbones and the inside of his teeth.

He threw again. High. Wild. His own fault. Ball two.

The Arbiter's call snapped like a ruler on a desk. "Two and oh."

"Throw," Jerry signaled. No visit. No extra word.

Dock exhaled and threw a fastball straight down the middle, not clever, not pretty, just a challenge.

The ball crossed the plate, white and honest.

"Ball three," the Arbiter said.

The batter blinked. So did Jerry. The crowd grumbled, a low roll of confusion.

Dock stepped off the mound and stared toward the plate.

"That was there," he said.

The Arbiter tilted his head. "You are not in charge of where here is."

Dock's fingers tightened around the ball. For a heartbeat he wanted to walk in from the mound, pull the mask off with both hands, and show the whole stadium what he was talking to.

Instead, he stepped back on the rubber.

Three and oh. No hitter on the line. Reality on the line. He lifted, threw, and fired as hard as his arm would allow.

The batter never swung. The pitch caught nothing but center.

"Strike one," the Arbiter called.

The tone was amused. Not mockery. Amusement, pure and thin.

Dock laughed once, a dry bark. The batter shook his head and reset, clearly rattled by the moving target.

Three and one. Dock dropped a curve that started at the shoulder and finished at the shoelaces. The man swung right through it.

Three and two.

Jerry's glove did not move for the next sign. High and in. Finish him.

Dock felt the seams bite his fingertips. He let the pitch go.

The ball rose into the man's hands, scorching inches off the wood. The swing was late, cramped, angry.

The bat found nothing.

"Strike three," the Arbiter snapped.

The batter cursed, tossed his bat too hard, and stalked back to the dugout. He glared at the plate umpire as if the man were ordinary. The Arbiter did not look at him once.

One out.

The shape over the moon shifted.

Dock caught it in the corner of his eye. To anyone else it was just a thin cloud bank, a gray smear crossing silver. To him it was mass. It was intent.

It grew.

The second hitter stepped in and the stadium lights dimmed by a fraction, just enough for Dock's shadow to lengthen.

The Arbiter's mask vibrated, metal that had never been metal. The black around his face deepened until it was no longer color at all. It was absence. It was hallway, not surface.

"Do you want to see it?" he asked.

Dock swallowed. "I have seen plenty."

"No," the Arbiter said. "You have seen incidents. You have seen effects. You have not seen who counts them."

The dirt at home plate cracked. Just a hairline at first, like dried mud. Then it widened, a black thread that ran from the catcher's cleats out toward the mound, then sidelong toward first, then back across like a lightning pattern drawn by a slow hand.

The crack did not cut the chalk. It followed it.

The white lines bowed as the earth flexed. They did not break. They bent.

The batter did not notice. He dug in, tapping the plate once.

Dock came set and fired. Another strike. Swing and miss. The man cursed, shook his head, reset.

The crack widened.

Something moved beneath the plate. Not a shape, not yet. A presence, thick and patient.

"You should have walked off in the second," the Arbiter said. "You still had your excuses then. Time lost. Phone call. Rotation. Chemicals you dropped under your tongue. You could have spent the rest of your life telling yourself it would have been different."

"Too late for that," Dock said.

"Yes," the Arbiter replied. "Too late for that."

The second pitch slid inside and clipped cloth. The batter jerked away and glared, but the ball had never touched him. Dock knew it. Jerry knew it.

"Ball one," the Arbiter said, pleasant as a bank teller.

"You like this," Dock said quietly.

The Arbiter's shoulders moved. It might have been a shrug. It might have been some other motion entirely.

"I like the record," he said. "What men like you call fairness. I like that it keeps you busy."

Dock threw another curve. The ball danced, lost speed, climbed, then dropped like the floor had been taken away from under it. The hitter swung through dust.

Strike two.

The crack under home plate split.

It did not burst open. It unfolded, like a seam unthreading. The clay parted in a long, slow sigh, and something slid through.

It was black at first. Not just color, but the absence of reflection. Then it changed. Lines of faint light ran along its surface, like chalk diagrams of angles and arcs. It rose higher, and Dock realized it was not a single thing. It was many small cords twisted together, each one thick as a man's leg, each one looping back on itself.

Tentacles.

Not wet. Not slick. Not squid. These were tendrils of rule and measure. Every surface carried tiny notches, like hash marks cut into a tally stick. As they moved, the marks shifted, reordering into columns and rows.

They slid up past the catcher's back and through the Arbiter's chest protector without disturbing the fabric. They did not emerge from him. They passed through him, as though he were a lens.

The stands did not scream. The crowd did not flinch. To them, nothing had happened.

To Dock, the whole backstop was now the edge of a wound.

The Arbiter's voice stayed calm. "This is the part behind the mask. The reason you get only four balls, three strikes, ninety feet, sixty feet six inches. The reason a line can be fair on one side and foul on the other. It was built to hold something in place. And you keep throwing the ball at it."

The batter half stepped out, unsettled by Dock's stare.

"Time," he said.

The Arbiter did not grant it.

"Get back in," the plate umpire said out loud, his human voice finally appearing. The player grumbled and returned to the box.

Dock's chest felt tight. His eyes burned. The tentacles above the plate unfurled further, higher, splitting into more cords that reached up toward the lights. They brushed the bulbs and the bulbs dimmed.

From the upper rim of the stadium, concrete groaned. A shadow slid across the outfield wall, independent of the bodies that cast it.

Jerry flashed the fingers for a fastball and did not look up once.

Dock took a breath that tasted like dirt and old fear.

He threw.

The batter swung and chopped a weak grounder toward second. For a heartbeat Dock saw two balls rolling, then four, then none, then one again. Mazeroski floated smoothly into motion, took it clean, and threw out the runner with a snap of the wrist. Routine, on paper.

The Arbiter nodded once. "Two away."

The tentacles rose higher.

They breached the plane of the stadium roof, but Dock could still see them as clearly as the glove in front of him. They climbed taller and taller, thickening, branching, until they overshadowed the lights entirely. At the top, they twisted together and hinted at a form that was not human and not animal.

He glimpsed a vast circle, then a set of ridges that might have been teeth or might have been bleachers seen from the wrong side of reality. Between them, a hole opened and shut, quietly, like a throat taking slow breaths.

The third hitter stepped in and spit.

He looked so small. His gray Padres uniform sagged slightly at the belt. His bat looked too heavy for his hands.

"You cannot win," the Arbiter said.

"Scoreboard says different," Dock replied.

"The scoreboard is a child's toy," the voice said. "What I keep never fits on that board."

Dock wiped his wrist across his mouth and tasted salt and copper.

"Then why play it at all," he asked.

"Because you are simple," the Arbiter answered. "You need chunks. Nine innings. Fifty years. One body, one life. You could not live inside the whole count. You would scream until your throat broke. So we give you seasons. We give you games. You tell yourselves that what happens here is separate."

A tentacle brushed along the right field foul pole. The metal rang for a heartbeat with no wind touching it.

Dock came set again.

"Go home," the Arbiter said. "Let the ball drop. Let the hit fall in front of Clemente. He will forgive you. The line will close and I will be what I have always been. The catcher will remember you were wild. The newspapers will remember you were strange. The no hitter will never exist. You will live a little longer in your own head."

Dock felt something cold coil behind his heart.

The offer was real. That was the worst part. He could feel the branch of reality it would grow into. A simple single to center. A manager's slow walk. A shrug and a shower.

He saw himself five years later, telling the story as a barroom anecdote, the night he almost, the day the acid ran faster than his arm. He heard laughter, saw hands clapping his shoulder. He watched himself live a little softer.

"No," Dock said.

The Arbiter's mask tilted. "You will regret that."

"I regret a lot," Dock said. "Not this."

He drove the next pitch at the bottom of the zone. The hitter did not even swing. His face went slack, eyes too wide, as if he had finally heard a bit of the voice that had been talking only to the man on the mound.

"Strike one," the Arbiter called.

Another fastball, same spot. Swing and miss. A full yard behind.

"Strike two."

The tentacles above the stadium clenched. The whole mass tightened, twisting around an invisible core. The shape they formed hovered between structure and chaos, like someone had tried to build a cathedral out of muscle and scar tissue.

Dock felt a pressure behind his eyes, as if someone were pushing his head inward from all sides.

"Do you know why you hurt boys by rivers," the Arbiter asked. "Why men fall on motel balconies. Why a crowd burns its own houses while uniforms march with clubs. You think these are random storms. They are not. They are relief valves. They keep you from tearing the whole fabric apart. Men like you who insist on seeing too much, we give you glimpses. Lynching in one decade, a riot in another, a rifle shot for a man in a tie. Small doses of what the world really is. Enough to terrify you. Not enough for you to act."

Dock saw the boy on the riverbank again, eyes bright in the flashlight beam. He saw the man on the stage bleeding into his palms. He saw the motel balcony, the brown print from his own hands on white sleeves.

He saw all of it and understood the cruelty of the pattern. The horror was not just the thing happening. The horror was the way it folded into history like another line in a ledger.

"Three," Jerry's fingers said.

Curve.

Dock rolled his shoulder once. His arm felt like something held together by stubbornness and tape.

He threw.

The curve started at the chest, tumbled forward, and fell off an unseen table that only ballplayers believed in. The hitter's bat traveled through empty space. His knees buckled. His mouth fell open.

"Strike three."

The inning was over.

The tentacles did not retract.

They continued to rise.

By the time Dock reached the dugout rail, the creature above the stadium had taken a fuller shape. It was not a body in the way humans understood bodies. It was an arrangement of functions. A central mass, enormous and circular, ringed with layers of moving ridges that opened and closed in slow alternation. Each ridge carried small lights, thousands of them, blinking in a rhythm that never quite repeated. The tentacles rose from the underside and sank through the roof of the stadium into the dirt, into the stands, into the concrete decks where fans ate hot dogs and drank beer.

He realized that the cords in the dugout ceiling had been part of it. The drip that crawled along Osborn's crack of concrete. The hiss in the bullpen phone. The line between sidewalk and squad car. It had been here all day, all his life, counting by rules he had never been allowed to write.

Teammates slapped his shoulder. Mazeroski said something about staying down in the zone. Stargell talked about adding one more run so Dock could breathe. Clemente said nothing, but his eyes did more than any hand on a shoulder.

At the far end of the bench, Don Osborn watched the sky.

He did not look away when Dock sat near his feet, breathing hard.

"You see it," Dock said.

Osborn's jaw worked the stub of a cigar that had long since gone out. "I see cracks."

"That thing," Dock said. "Behind the lights."

Osborn kept his gaze upward. "I have seen worse."

Dock almost laughed. "You calling that ordinary."

"I am calling it old," Osborn said. "The world had rules before baseball did. Those rules ate people. This just counts them."

Dock followed his eyes. "You afraid."

"Of it," Osborn said. "No. Of what you might do to it. Maybe."

Bartirome pressed new liniment into Dock's shoulder, his hands gentle and firm.

"Two more," the trainer said.

"Three," Dock corrected. "I still got to get through eight."

Bartirome shrugged. "In my head, you are already in the ninth."

Top of the eighth passed like a dream. A grounder, a flyout, a strikeout that wasted another Padre. The Pirates did not score. They did not need to, numbers wise. The game was already in Dock's hands whether he wanted it or not.

The eighth inning came and went like something half remembered from a dream. Dock faced three men and none of them felt real. One lined out softly to short. One swung at a pitch that seemed to veer sideways the moment it left his hand. One stood frozen as the Arbiter called a strike that had no business being a strike.

When Dock returned to the dugout, the scoreboard showed eight innings gone. He could not recall a single pitch of it. He only felt that the thing above the stadium had stopped watching and had begun waiting.

Murtaugh clapped him once on the shoulder. Clemente murmured something about three more. Stargell told him to breathe.

Dock stepped over the foul line again. His leg brushed the chalk and it hissed like something alive.

The bottom of the ninth began in a silence that felt too loud.

The first batter walked on four pitches, none of them close. Dock's arm rebelled, the pressure in his skull pulling his mechanics apart thread by thread. His fingers tingled, then went numb. The runner at first looked back with the faint smile of a man who knew he had not earned the gift and intended to take it anyway.

Jerry thumped his mitt and walked out.

He did not say that Dock was fine.
He said, "Stay here. Do not go up there."

Dock knew what he meant. His eyes had drifted back to the thing above the stadium.

"I cannot ignore it," Dock said.

"You do not have to ignore it," Jerry said. "You just do not pitch to it. You pitch to me. That is all you ever do. You throw it at the glove. The rest of this is none of our business."

The second batter squared to bunt. Dock let the first pitch ride up and in. The batter flinched back and stared out with something like suspicion or fear or both.

Dock set, threw again, and the Padres hitter showed bunt too early. The ball kicked straight up off the bat, a weak pop no higher than the brim of his helmet. Dock lost it in the lights. Jerry did not. He tore off the mask, tracked the wobble, and slid on his knees to cradle it against his chest before it could touch dirt.

One out. No hits. One man on.

The crowd came alive. Padres fans found their throats. Pirates fans tensed.

Above it all the tentacles tightened.

The third batter stepped in. His hands shook. He did not know what he was inside.

Dock threw him four pitches. None found the zone. Whether that was Dock's arm or the Arbiter's hand on the threads of the world, he could not say.

Walk.

A murmur rolled through the stands. The creature pulsed once, a ripple of approval that shivered through the lights and metal.

The fourth batter took a curve in the dirt and a fastball off the edge. Two and nothing.

Jerry walked in again.

"Look at me," he said.

Dock did.

"What do you see," Jerry asked.

"Stone," Dock said.

"Good. Because that is all I am. I am not God. I am not that thing up there. I am a man in gear. If you throw it where I tell you, we get three more. I do not care what is happening behind my back."

He slapped the ball into Dock's glove with more force than usual.

"Do not give it the hit. If the world wants to be the way it is, let it be. You hold this one thing."

He turned and went back.

Dock focused on the tape on Jerry's fingers. The square of target. The cleats in the dirt. The runner's shadow stretching off first.

He threw a strike.

He threw another.

The batter chopped the next pitch toward short, a sharp one hopper that looked ordinary and felt like a sentence. Alley stayed low, fielded clean, and flipped to Maz. For a heartbeat the entire universe hung on the pivot at second.

Maz caught, touched the bag, turned, and fired.

Oliver smothered it. Double play.

Two outs. Bases empty. One man to go.

The crowd exploded. Pirates players pounded the rail. The Padres slumped. Above it all the creature shuddered.

Lights along its rim blinked in chaotic patterns. The tentacles writhed, tightening around an invisible core. It was not rage. It was adjustment. A system scrambling to correct for an outcome it did not prefer and could not forbid.

"Last batter," the Arbiter said.

Dock felt sweat running down his spine. His fingers were slick inside the glove. His heartbeat had gone from drum to hammer.

The final hitter stepped in. A bench player with a sagging jersey and a stance a little too wide. He looked like a man who knew his name would not appear in very many books.

Unless he broke this one thing.

"Walk him," the Arbiter said. "Hit him. Call Murtaugh and tell him your arm is gone. Take the mercy yourself. Do not make me keep letting you play."

Dock thought of all the times mercy had been offered to his people with a smile and a gun behind it.

"Fuck you," he said.

The first pitch sailed high. Ball one. The roar from the stands stirred the creature's flesh. It rippled like a pond shaken by stones.

The second pitch clipped the outside edge. The hitter stared, half expecting a call and half expecting a gift.

"Ball two," the Arbiter said.

Dock grinned, humorless. "You really want that hit. You're not getting' it, man."

"I want the pattern," the Arbiter said. "You are a noisy outlier. A man like you is supposed to be managed. A troubled arm. A temper. An early exit. It fits the shape. A miracle game does not."

The third pitch caught too much plate. The hitter swung and fouled it back.

Two and one.

The ball rose straight into the sky, struck the belly of the creature, and vanished. Dock saw a light blink on along its rim. That moment would be recorded. Not as a stat. As data for whatever the thing was building.

He set again.

The fourth pitch was a fastball down. The hitter swung over it.

Two and two.

The no hitter stood on a thin edge. Clemente shifted in right. Stargell settled in left. Maz bent his knees. Everyone understood that if the world wanted to be cruel, this was the place it would choose.

The Arbiter waited.

Dock felt every bad thing he had ever done. Every time he had mouthed off to a coach. Every woman he had let down. Every night he had chased a high because the day had failed him. They all lined up and stared at him, waiting for him to prove them right.

He thought of Clemente's words.

You play like a man fighting God.

Maybe so.

Jerry held up his glove. No sign. No number. Just faith.

Dock gripped the ball. The seams fit his fingers like a lock accepting a key.

He chose a pitch that should not have worked. A rising fastball on a tired arm. Something thrown in defiance of physics.

He lifted. He stepped. He turned his hips and let the chain of motion travel bone to bone, muscle to muscle, into his shoulder, his elbow, his wrist.

He let the ball go.

For a second it did not move.

The stadium froze. The tentacles held still. The crowd's noise cut off. The creature's maw opened wide enough to swallow the field whole.

The ball hung in the seam between two worlds.

Then time stuttered back.

The pitch climbed. It did not fade. It rode the line Dock needed, not the one the book prescribed.

The hitter swung.

The bat cut under it by the width of a stitch.

The ball snapped into Jerry's mitt.

Silence, for a heartbeat.

Then the Arbiter said, in both voices at once, "Strike three."

The sound cracked through Dock's skull and through the creature above. The tentacles convulsed. Lights along the rim burst in white flashes. The central mass shuddered, then collapsed inward.

The thing did not die.

It folded.

It folded the way the sky had folded when Dock left the mound earlier.

It folded like paper being tucked into a smaller shape, meant to be stored until the next time it was hungry.

It dragged its cords out of the stands, the dirt, the chalk. It slipped into the tear at home plate and vanished, leaving the air trembling like a wound that refused to close.

The crowd erupted.

Stargell rushed from left. Maz and Oliver converged. Clemente jogged in with the quiet certainty of a man who already knew the result. They swallowed Dock on the grass, pounding his back, grabbing his cap.

He heard none of it.

He felt only the seam of the world, still hot beneath his

spikes, glowing like something that wanted to be touched again.

The Arbiter stepped onto the mound as if rising from inside the dirt. No one else saw him. The mask was plain again. The pads looked cheap again. Only the eyes stayed wrong.

"You proved something," he said.

Dock nodded once, jaw tight. "Yeah. Proved I could throw with the whole sky leaning on my arm."

"You proved the rules bind me too," the Arbiter said. "I do not like that."

"You remember everything," Dock said.

"Yes. And that is the only mercy you will ever have. You will not be forgotten. You will also not be spared." The Arbiter's voice thickened, as if another voice were trying to speak through the first.

Dock felt his knees soften, but he forced himself upright again. "You talk like you won something."

"I kept the shape intact," the Arbiter said. "You do not understand what that costs."

Dock stepped toward him. "I understand plenty. I understand you tried to break me. I understand you bent the field to make me fold. I understand you wanted me to hand it over so you could write your neat little story."

The Arbiter's head tilted. "What happens to you now is not mine to soften."

Dock spat in the dirt. "Never asked you to soften a thing."

The Arbiter leaned in, close enough that Dock felt cold through the heat still rising off the mound. "Game is over."

Dock did not step back. "For you," he said, and the words came out low and sharp, stripped of any fear. "Not for me. Not for men like me. You get to vanish into whatever hole you crawled out of and tally your moments. I have to walk back into a world full of hands that look just like yours. They do not wear masks. They do not need to. They follow rules too. Their own."

The Arbiter's eyes flickered. Something behind him shivered in the dirt, thin and hungry, waiting to be called.

"Your fight continues," he said.

"It has always continued," Dock replied. "You were just the first one big enough to show your face."

For the first time, the Arbiter hesitated. The mask shifted, not physically, but in the way some expressions shift inside shadow.

"You think you changed anything," he said.

"I changed you," Dock said.

The Arbiter took a single slow step back, as if measuring the space between them. "You will not win outside these lines."

"I already did," Dock said. "You just watched it."

The Arbiter's body dimmed, outline thinning. "We will meet again. The beginning always returns."

Dock lifted his chin. "Then start praying I do not throw like this next time."

The Arbiter paused at the edge of the mound, half real and half something else. "The shape will find you," he said.

Dock met his stare. "So will I."

The Arbiter dissolved into the thin seam of shadow between two blades of grass, as quiet and inevitable as a thought a man tries not to think.

His teammates still mobbed him. Murtaugh smiled a thin, proud smile. Clemente's eyes were steady and heavy with understanding.

"Well," Clemente said. "You did it."

"Did I," Dock asked.

"For tonight," Clemente answered.

The Arbiter walked toward the tunnel. Before he disappeared, he paused.

"That is enough for one game," he said.

Dock heard the other meaning.

Not enough for a life.

The scoreboard shone simple truth:

PADRES 0

PIRATES 2

NO HITS

Dock's vision blurred. His legs buckled. Someone caught him under the arms. For a second he thought it was the tentacles again.

It was Stargell and Maz, laughing and shouting.

The world tilted, then went black.

He fell, not through air, but through a seam he could not see.

The last thing he heard was the crowd's roar fading into a static hiss, then nothing at all, as if someone had turned the volume down on the entire planet.

Then there was only silence, and the faint memory of the Arbiter's voice repeating a sentence that had no end:

You always end where you begin.

Chapter Twelve

The Game is Over

Dock woke to the sound of water.

Not waves this time. Showers. Pipes thudding in the walls. Drains sucking at the floor. The air smelled like liniment, sweat, beer, and wet wool. Light bled in from a row of bare bulbs, too bright and too steady for his eyes.

He was on a training table. Someone had put a towel under his head. Another lay over his chest. His arm tingled from shoulder to wrist, not in the hot-wire way of the mound, but in the dull buzzing of muscles figuring out they were still attached.

"Welcome back."

Bartirome sat on a rolling stool beside him, tape still looped around two fingers. He looked like he had never moved. Only the new creases in his shirt said time had passed.

Dock tried to sit up. His body did not agree. The room tipped, then steadied. "What happened?"

"You dropped," Tony said. "Out there on the grass. Right after they mobbed you."

The word 'they' arrived with a smile. Not mockery. Something close to pride.

"Mobbed me," Dock repeated. His voice sounded wrong to his own ears, both far away and too close.

Tony nodded toward the open doorway that led to the locker room. "You threw the no hitter. You remember that part, or do I need to write it on your forehead?"

Images came back in pieces. The last pitch. The ball hanging in the air. Jerry's glove. The sound of the call. The creature above the lights folding in on itself like a wound closing. His knees quitting.

"I remember," Dock said.

"Good." Tony checked one of Dock's pupils with a small penlight. "You scared the hell out of a lot of people. Osborn wanted to put you on a stretcher. Murtaugh told him if you can walk to the bus, you can ride it. You get about five minutes before he comes in here asking why you are still horizontal."

"How long was I out?"

"Couple of minutes. Maybe more." Tony shrugged. "Time gets funny in a clubhouse after a game like that."

Noise drifted in. Laughter, metal lockers slamming, spikes scraping on concrete. Someone singing off-key. Someone else telling the same story again, a little louder, a little better.

"Anybody tell me what I looked like from the outside," Dock asked. "On the mound, I mean."

Tony pursed his lips. "Wild as hell. Untouchable anyway. Walked enough guys to fill a bus. No hits. Six strikeouts. One hit batsman. You already know the line. You were there."

That last sentence hung between them.

"Yeah," Dock said softly. "I was there."

Tony watched him another second, then patted his calf. "Congratulations, Dock. Whatever else, they can't take that line out of the book."

He rose, bones cracking, and moved toward the lockers.

Dock lay still. The overhead bulb hummed. Water thundered behind the tiled wall. His arm felt like it belonged to someone else.

He slid off the table. His legs protested. He stood anyway. The floor was cool under his feet. The concrete felt ordinary. No pulse. No breath.

In the mirror above the sink, his reflection looked like a man who had been dragged behind a truck for three hours and then asked to smile for a picture. His eyes were red and raw. His lip was swollen. There was a welt at his hairline he did not remember getting.

He half expected to see a mask behind him in the glass. Bars. Black shell. Dishwater eyes.

The mirror showed only the room. The towel on the table. The door to the showers. A row of hooks with uniforms dripping from them. His own face staring back, trying not to flinch.

He splashed water on his cheeks. It was lukewarm and tasted like metal.

Voices grew louder. A burst of laughter, then applause, then the crack of a champagne cork. Someone shouted his name.

Dock stepped into the locker room.

Stargell saw him first. He threw both arms high and hollered the line in a triumphant Hendrix howl, *"Standing next to a mountain, chop it down with the edge of my hand..."* He pointed straight at Dock, grinning wide. "That is you tonight, brother. Dock Ellis, MISTER Untouchable!"

The whole room turned. For a second Dock thought they all had the same face. Then they resolved into teammates again. Maz. Oliver. Alley. Robertson. Manny. Even the rookies who had barely gotten off the bench looked like they had been waiting all night for this doorway to fill.

Somebody handed him a paper cup. It brimmed with something fizzy and cheap that claimed to be champagne. It smelled like sugar and the back of a bus.

Murtaugh stepped forward, hand out. His cap sat low. His jaw clenched in what might have been a smile or might have been an attempt to smoke three cigarettes at once without setting the lineup card on fire.

"Hell of a game, Ellis" he said. "You did your job."

Dock took the hand. It was dry and strong and did not shake. "Almost didn't," he said.

"Almost doesn't print," Murtaugh replied. "Two runs for us. None for them. No hits. That is what goes down. After that, you and God can argue about the rest."

The manager moved on. Reporters hovered near the doorway, notebooks ready, tape recorders in hand. They waited like vultures who had been told to wear ties.

Stargell slung an arm around Dock's shoulders. "You scared them, you know that," he said. "They wanted you out of there in the fifth. Sixth at the latest. Skip told them no. Said if you were going to kill us, you would have done it by now."

Dock managed a laugh. "That supposed to make me feel loved.?"

"That is the closest you get," Stargell said. "You feel anything right now?"

Dock thought about the ball in his hand. The world under his feet. The thing above the lights. He thought about the Arbiter's voice in his skull like a thumb on a bruise.

"Tired," he said.

Stargell snorted. "Good. Means you did it right. Get dressed before the writers start writing the story without you."

They did anyway.

Reporters circled. Questions came in quick, sharp bursts. "Did you know you had no hits allowed?" "When did you realize the history at stake?" "Was this the best you have ever had your stuff?" "How did you bear down with all those walks?"

He gave them quotes that sounded like they belonged in a morning paper. Stuff about eating innings, saving the bullpen arms, trusting his catcher, throwing what May called. He did not tell them about the tentacles. He did not tell them about the boy in the river or the man on the balcony. He did not tell them about the creature that lived under the chalk and counted every breath.

A young reporter, hair parted clean and tie too tight, asked, "You think tonight proves something to your critics. The ones who say you are more talk than production."

Dock looked at him a little too long. "I think it proves I got them out," he said. "That is what pitchers do. They get them out."

The kid flushed, scribbling anyway.

Another reporter, older, white hair curling past his collar, tried for a softer angle. "Some people will say a night like this wipes the slate. Fresh start, clean page. Does it feel like redemption to you, Dock?"

He thought of the Arbiter saying 'you will not be spared.'

He thought of Officer Braddock with his mirrored shades. Of the PA voice in the terminal splitting the airport into zones of color. Of every time he had been watched for how he stood, how he spoke, how he dressed.

"Slate never fresh for us," Dock said. "You write on what they give you."

The man blinked. "Could you repeat that."

"No," Dock said.

The questions dwindled. The reporters peeled away, chasing other quotes, other deadlines. The champagne went flat. The room emptied in waves. Equipment guys carried hampers toward the truck. Trainers gathered towels. The noise settled into the clink of lockers and the low murmur of men getting ready to leave.

Clemente sat at his locker in a clean shirt, tie knotted neat, hair still damp at the temples. He waited while Dock pulled on slacks and a button-down, each motion slower than it needed to be.

"You remember the game?" Clemente asked.

"Most of it," Dock said.

"The part that matters," Clemente said. "You know what they will write. Wild. Brilliant. Something about your temper. Something about a second chance you did not ask them for."

Dock tugged on his shoes. The leather felt tight across his toes. "You sound like you have seen this before."

"I read," Clemente said. "And I live here. That is enough."

He leaned forward, elbows on knees. "They will talk about tonight like it is a miracle. Black, troublemaking pitcher throws a no hitter. They will pat themselves on the back for watching it. For cheering you. For clapping in the right place. Tomorrow some of them will sit on a committee and vote to keep a school district the way it is. In a week a cop will stop you again for walking the wrong way."

"Already did that," Dock said.

Clemente nodded. "And it will keep happening. They will put numbers by your name in the book. They will not put numbers by those things. They are not errors to them. They are how the game is kept in order."

Dock swallowed. "Then why do it. Why throw it at all."

Clemente looked at him, steady. "Because a man does his duty. Haz tu deber siempre. You cannot fix the book. You can write your own line in it. Sometimes that is enough to carry someone else a little further. Maybe not you. Maybe a boy somewhere who looks at that box score and sees what is possible and what is not yet finished."

"You think that boy will be watching this game," Dock asked.

"If he is lucky," Clemente said. "Or if he is cursed. It is hard to tell the difference out here."

He stood. "Sleep if you can. Drink water. Tomorrow they will ask you the same questions again. Try to tell the truth without letting them use it against you."

"You make that sound like stealing home," Dock said.

Clemente almost smiled. "Harder," he said. "Good night, Dock."

"Night, Bobby."

The clubhouse emptied. The shouts moved out to the hallway, then to the bus, then away. The hum of the lights grew louder. Somewhere a television crackled in the trainers' room, sound turned low.

Dock sat alone in front of his locker.

On the bench next to him lay a baseball. Someone had written on it in thick black marker.

JUNE 12, 1970
SAN DIEGO 0
PITTSBURGH 2
NO HITTER
DOCK ELLIS

He picked it up.

In his hand it was only leather and yarn and cork. No pulse. No heat. The seams felt raised but not alive. He closed his fingers around it anyway.

"You feel dead now," he muttered. "Good. You had enough life for two nights."

He put the ball gently in his travel bag, between a clean shirt and a pair of socks with a hole in the heel.

On the way out, he passed pitching coach Don Osborn standing near the door, cap still pulled low, hands in his pockets. The old coach looked at him the way a man looks at a structure after an earthquake, checking for cracks.

"You see all of it," Dock asked.

Osborn tilted his head. "I saw enough. Saw you pitch out of things you had no business getting out of. Saw the stat line. That is my job. I am not here to read the other stuff."

"There was other stuff," Dock said.

"I know," Osborn replied. "There always is. I live in the part where the ball leaves your hand and then arrives somewhere. The rest belongs to whoever wrote the rules. I just teach you to live inside them as long as you can."

Dock frowned. "You believe in that. The rules."

Osborn's eyes crinkled. "I believe they exist. Belief is not agreement. You get them to bend a little tonight. That is all a pitcher ever does. Put his fingers on the stitch and twist, make something that wants to go straight move another way. You did that. Remember how it felt. One day you will not be able to. Then you will need the memory."

He stepped aside. "Bus is waiting, Ellis. They won't hold it, not even for you."

The bus ride to the hotel was quiet. Men dozed into their jackets. A few talked in low voices about plays, about swings, about hotels in other towns. Someone in the back argued softly about music, saying Berry Gordy had built an empire but crushed plenty of people on the way up, and that everyone knew it even if they kept playing his records.

Outside the windows the city slipped past. Streetlights slid over Dock's face in regular pulses. Every so often he thought he saw a shape above the freeway, something large and slow moving that kept pace with the bus without sound. Every time he blinked and looked again, it was gone.

The hotel room was cold and beige and smelled faintly of old cigarettes and stronger disinfectant. A generic painting of a sailboat hung over the bed, its water painted the wrong color for San Diego. The curtains did not quite meet in the middle. Streetlight pushed through the gap and laid a yellow blade across the carpet.

Dock dropped his bag, sat on the edge of the bed, and stared at the television set on its low rolling stand.

He did not remember turning it on.

The screen glowed anyway.

The image was black and white, flat and clean. Outfield grass in gray stripes. Uniforms washed to the same dull tone. The picture wobbled once, then steadied. A graphic slid onto the bottom corner.

PIRATES VS PADRES
JUNE 12, 1970
REPLAY

The sound came in with a soft hiss. The familiar voice of the local play-by-play man floated through the room, excited but controlled.

"Welcome back to our special delayed broadcast of tonight's historic contest at San Diego Stadium. For those of you just joining us, you are in for something extra. Dock Ellis is on the mound for the Pirates and is, well, working on a little something special."

Dock's skin prickled.

He watched himself on the screen. The man in gray and black looked like him, moved like him, jerked at the cap the way he always did between pitches. The mechanics looked wild, but not otherworldly. No tentacles under his spikes. No shudder in the air above the lights. Only a pitcher with too much energy and a fastball he sometimes pointed into the dirt by mistake.

He watched the second inning. The third. Walks showed up as high pitches, misses off the plate. The umpire on the screen called balls and strikes without drama. The strike zone looked tight, but ordinary. When Dock had heard humming and giggles, the tape offered nothing but the usual barked calls and the occasional dusting of the plate.

He waited to see the sky split. The stadium on screen remained intact concrete and metal. The crowd stayed in their seats, fanning themselves with scorecards.

He watched Clemente's throw from right. The ball did not glow. It cut across the frame in one beautiful straight line, glove to glove, runner out by a step. The announcer nearly shouted himself hoarse.

He watched Stargell's home run. The camera followed the ball into darkness, then cut to Willie's smile as he rounded second. No lights flickered. No shape moved over the moon. The replay showed only a night game, a deep drive, a scoreboard number ticking from one to two.

The broadcast jumped ahead. "We take you now," the announcer said, "to the bottom of the ninth here in San Diego, where Dock Ellis is three outs away from making history."

The image shifted. Dock saw himself again on the mound. His shoulders looked tighter now. His cap shadowed his eyes. Jerry May crouched behind the plate, target square and solid.

The first batter. Four wild pitches, none in the strike zone. A walk. The announcer commented on nerves, on fatigue, on the pressure of the moment.

The second hitter squared to bunt, then pulled back. On television, the weak pop to the catcher looked almost comical, a nothing play. Jerry's slide and basket catch brought a cheer. One out. No mention of tentacles or threats.

The third batter chopped a ball to short. The camera framed Alley's fielding, Maz's turn at second, Oliver's stretch at first. Double play. The inning ended with textbook neatness. The picture lingered on Dock's reaction.

On the screen, his arms went up. Teammates swarmed him. Caps flew. The crowd rose.

The view cut to the press box camera, high above the plate. From there the field looked like a diagram. The mound, the plate, the lines, all in their proper places.

The announcer's voice grew almost reverent. "He has done it. Dock Ellis has completed the no hitter, pitching himself out of jams, walking eight batters, striking out six, and facing hurdles only he can truly understand. But that is it. He has done it. The game is over."

The picture froze on Dock's face, half buried in a pile of gray uniforms.

Dock looked at the screen.

"Game is over," the man on television said again, softer this time, as if tasting the words.

Dock listened to the air conditioner huff against the window. A car horn bleated somewhere far below. Someone laughed in the hallway.

He let the sentence sit between him and the screen.

"Game is over."

He heard Braddock's voice in it. Heard the airport PA. Heard the Arbiter. Heard every time someone had told him that one good performance, one good deed, one clean stat line made everything square.

He leaned forward, elbows on his knees, and spoke to the empty room.

"Game ain't over," he said. "Not really."

On the television, the frozen image of the umpire behind the plate looked back at him. For a heartbeat, the black of the mask seemed deeper than the rest of the picture. The bars caught a light that was not there. The eyes behind it did not exist on film, but Dock felt them on him anyway.

He got up and walked to the set. His reflection hovered in the glass, superimposed over the still frame of his own celebration. For a second, he saw both Dock Ellises at once. The man on the field, successful, perfect for one night, lifted by teammates. The man in the hotel, alone in socks and a shirt he had not fully buttoned, speaking to a machine.

Between them, in the faint ghost of the glass, he thought he saw another shape. A hint of black shell, a curve of chest protector, a clicker in a gloved hand.

He blinked.

Only his own face remained.

The broadcast resumed, spilling highlights, postgame quotes, a smiling shot of Murtaugh saying something about guts and grit. Dock turned the volume down until the room was filled only with moving mouths and no sound.

He sat on the bed and stared at the picture without hearing it. A graphic rolled past with the final line:

SAN DIEGO 0 0 0
PITTSBURGH 2 3 0

He thought of all the other lines that would never be written. Every stop and frisk. Every redlined block. Every closed door that did not say no out loud but meant it all the same. He thought of Emmett Till at the river. Of Malcolm on the stage. Of Martin on the balcony. Of the boy with tape on his knuckles running past the burning storefront in his vision.

The Arbiter had gone wherever it went when the lights were off and the stands were empty. The creature above the stadium had folded itself invisible again. The rules were still there. You could not see gravity either, but it did not stop working when the inning ended.

He lay back, shoes still on, and watched the ceiling. The plaster was cracked in one corner. It made a small branching pattern, like a river system viewed from too high up, or like veins in a hand.

He closed his eyes.

He saw stitches.

He saw the line of a throw. He saw a boy somewhere, years from now, opening a sports page and running his finger down the column until it landed on his name. Dock Ellis, 9.0 IP, 0 H, 8 BB, 6 K.

He hoped the boy would feel pride first. Then anger. Then something hard that would not let him settle for just being written down as a pleasant anomaly in someone else's book.

Sleep came in ugly fits. He woke more than once, sure he had heard a clicker counting somewhere in the room. Every time he sat up, breath held, the only sound was the air conditioner and the low traffic outside.

In the morning the papers called it brilliant and bizarre. One headline used the word erratic. Another hinted at "off field distractions" without naming any. One column spent more ink on his clothes and hair than on his pitches.

On page thirteen of one paper, below the fold, there was a small article about a Black teenager in another city shot by police who said they thought the boy had a gun. He had not. There was no box score under his name. Only a brief paragraph and the promise of an investigation.

Dock folded the paper and put it in the trash.

That afternoon, as the team packed to travel, a clubhouse attendant taped a photocopy of the box score above his locker. Teammates signed it, wrote messages in the margins. Wild thing. Hell of a night. You crazy. About time you finished one.

Clemente walked past, read it once, and said only, "They still lost. Remember that too."

"Who," Dock asked.

"The Padres," Clemente said. Then, after a beat, "And the rest of us."

He went out to the field to stretch.

Dock traced his own name on the smudged paper. For one night, in one place, against one team, inside one white chalk frame, he had beaten whatever watched him.

The rest of the scores were still coming in.

That night, somewhere far from San Diego, in another little room with another flickering screen, a different man would see something he was not supposed to see. A corner of the curtain. A seam in the sky. A rule behind a rule.

His story would not have a mound in it. It might have a factory or a courtroom or a church basement. The field would be different. The Arbiter would not.

The file with Dock Ellis's name on it settled into whatever cabinet such things lived in. It was not the last folder. It was not the first.

In the dark, between innings of history, something turned a page and looked for the next case.

Afterword

The game you just witnessed is over. That is what the record book will tell you.
It will say Dock Ellis walked off the mound in San Diego a victor.
It will say he threw nine innings without surrendering a single hit.
It will say the Pirates won two to nothing, and it will list every pitch by number and name.

The record book is tidy.
The record book is certain.
The record book has never been asked to explain anything larger than a score.

Outside those pages, the truth is rarely so polite.
There are men who spend their whole lives trying to prove they belong on a field that was not built for them. They throw their arms into knots, they grind their bones into dust, they play perfect games in imperfect worlds, and still they are asked for more. Dock Ellis learned something that night. Perfection changes the box score, but it does not change the country.

Maybe he pitched a miracle.
Maybe he pitched through a nightmare.
Maybe he saw something above that stadium that no cam-

era could catch.
Or maybe the world simply lifted its mask long enough for one man to glimpse the face beneath it.

Tomorrow the papers will say he made history.
Dock himself would tell you history has a way of repeating until someone forces it to stop.
The world will cheer him today and test him tomorrow. It always does.
Some games end with the final out. Others keep playing long after the lights go cold.

In time someone will open the tape of this night and see nothing unusual.
They will hear the announcer declare the no hitter complete and the game finished.
They will hear the line that wraps everything up neatly.
Game is over. That is what he says.
A voice snug inside the comfort of numbers and tradition.

But if you listen closely, you may hear the difference between ending and escape.
You may hear the space Dock left between two words.
You may hear the quiet truth he carried with him into the dark.

Game is over.
Not really.

The Dark Archives will remain open for those who care to look.
Stories do not end because the credits roll.
They wait.
They gather dust.
They live in the corners of stadiums and streets and countries that pretend not to hear them.

And somewhere, beyond a field that once held its breath, the sky is keeping count.

Until the next entry.

Further Reading & Resources

If you'd like to learn more about Dock Ellis, his career, and his life after baseball, the following articles, documentaries, and profiles are a great place to start:

- **"No No: A Dockumentary"** (2014) – Directed by Jeff Radice
  A powerful and humanizing look at Dock's life, not just the LSD game.
  (Available to stream on various platforms.)

- **"Dock Ellis's LSD No-Hitter and the History of Baseball's Trippiest Legend"**
  – *Rolling Stone*, by Jason Diamond
  https://www.rollingstone.com/culture/culture-sports/dock-ellis-lsd-no-hitter-baseball-history-1005871/

- **Dock Ellis Foundation** (founded in his honor):
  https://www.dockellisfoundation.org

Continues work in mental health, addiction support, and community care.

About the author

D. William Graves writes at the intersection of history, myth, and the unseen forces that shape ordinary lives. His work blends psychological tension with the quiet horrors embedded in American memory, often drawing on real events and forgotten truths to expose the shadows that linger beneath them.

Born in Tennessee and raised in a landscape where stories carry as much weight as fact, Graves developed an early fascination with the strange currents that run through everyday life. His fiction draws from that deep well, exploring the threads that bind a person to a moment, a place, or a country that does not always echo their name back to them kindly.

Before turning to fiction, he spent years studying the ways people tell their own stories: the official ones held in public record and the quieter ones carried in private. His writing asks what happens when those stories collide. What happens when the world blinks and the truth shows its teeth.

Seams of the Infinite is the first volume from the Dark Archives, a growing series of speculative tales that examine the borders of reality, the weight of identity, and the unseen machinery that turns behind the everyday.

Graves lives and writes in Tennessee.

www.ingramcontent.com/pod-product-compliance
Lightning Source LLC
Chambersburg PA
CBHW020045310726
48970CB00007B/2412